the Trace

SIX

    Zona de Silencio .............................................. 151

    Breakdown ................................................... 160

    The Tall Boy ................................................. 166

    Tres Generaciones ............................................ 168

    Night Soliloquy .............................................. 171

    Friday Morning .............................................. 175

SEVEN

    A Life Askance .............................................. 183

    A Bad Case .................................................. 186

    The Firing .................................................. 191

    A Vision .................................................... 194

    Hoa's Walk .................................................. 201

EIGHT

    Friday Evening .............................................. 205

    Friday Night ................................................ 209

    Hoa's Walk .................................................. 212

    Signs ....................................................... 214

    Hoa's Walk .................................................. 216

    Leaving the Cave ............................................ 218

    The Arroyo and Back......................................... 221

    Hoa's Turn .................................................. 229

    Sunday Morning ............................................. 235

EPILOGUE

    .......................................................... 243

the Trace

## also by Forrest Gander

FICTION
*As a Friend*

SELECTED POETRY
*Core Samples from the World*
*Deeds of Utmost Kindness*
*Eiko & Koma*
*Eye against Eye*
*Lynchburg*
*Redstart: An Ecological Poetics* (with John Kinsella)
*Science & Steepleflower*
*Torn Awake*

SELECTED TRANSLATIONS
*Firefly under the Tongue: Selected Poems of Coral Bracho*
*Fungus Skull Eye Wing: Selected Poems of Alfonso D'Aquino*
*The Night, by Jaime Saenz* (with Kent Johnson)
*Panic Cure: Poems from Spain for the 21st Century*
*Pinholes in the Night: Essential Poems from Latin America* (with Raúl Zurita)
*Rain of the Future: Poems by Valerie Mejer* (with Alexandra Zelman)
*Watchword, by Pura López Colomé*

ESSAYS
*A Faithful Existence: Reading, Memory & Transcendence*

# THE TRACE *a novel*

Forrest Gander

 A NEW DIRECTIONS BOOK

The publisher thanks Michael Friedman and Mark Shapiro for their assistance reading sections of this novel.

Manufactured in the United States of America
First published clothbound by New Directions in 2014.
New Directions Books are printed on acid-free paper.

*Library of Congress Cataloging-in-Publication Data*
Gander, Forrest, 1956–
The Trace : a novel / Forrest Gander.
pages cm
ISBN 978-0-8112-2371-3 (acid-free paper)
I. Title.
PS3557.A47T7 2014
813'.54—dc23                    2014007234

10  9  8  7  6  5  4  3  2  1

New Directions Books are published for James Laughlin
by New Directions Publishing Corporation
80 Eighth Avenue, New York 10011

*for Karin Gander*

*"This isn't a road. They said we'd find Tonaya on the other side of the ridge. But we've gone way past that ridge."*

—Juan Rulfo, "Can't You Hear the Dogs?"

# contents

**ONE**

La Esmeralda, Mexico .......................................... 5

**TWO**

Marfa, Texas ................................................. 11
Marfa Lights ................................................. 17
One Awake One Asleep ....................................... 21
Early Morning Run ........................................... 23
Marfa Cemetery .............................................. 29

**THREE**

Death of Bierce in Marfa ..................................... 37
Desert Music ................................................. 40
Snake on the Road ........................................... 46
Coming into Shafter .......................................... 55

**FOUR**

Crossing the Border into Ojinaga ............................. 69
La Esmeralda, Mexico ........................................ 80
Ojinaga to Presidio to Langtry ............................... 83
La Esmeralda ................................................. 89
Crossing the Border Again, Piedras Negras .................... 91
On the Road to Icamole ...................................... 94
La Hacienda de los Muertos .................................. 99
Desert Music ................................................. 109

**FIVE**

Death of Bierce in Icamole ................................... 113
Monclova to Ocampo ......................................... 116
Toward La Esmeralda ......................................... 124
Incident in La Esmeralda ..................................... 130
Death of Bierce in Sierra Mojada ............................ 136
Entre Chien et Loup .......................................... 143

SIX

Zona de Silencio .............................................. 151

Breakdown .................................................. 160

The Tall Boy ................................................ 166

Tres Generaciones ........................................... 168

Night Soliloquy ............................................. 171

Friday Morning .............................................. 175


SEVEN

A Life Askance .............................................. 183

A Bad Case ................................................. 186

The Firing ................................................. 191

A Vision ................................................... 194

Hoa's Walk ................................................. 201


EIGHT

Friday Evening .............................................. 205

Friday Night ................................................ 209

Hoa's Walk ................................................. 212

Signs ..................................................... 214

Hoa's Walk ................................................. 216

Leaving the Cave ............................................ 218

The Arroyo and Back ......................................... 221

Hoa's Turn ................................................. 229

Sunday Morning ............................................. 235


EPILOGUE

................................................................ 243

the Trace

*one*

*La Esmeralda, Mexico*

She knocked on the bathroom door.

"Can I come in to shower?"

"En el trono," he called out. "Give me a couple minutes."

He was just reaching for the roll of toilet paper on the floor when something happened. A reverberating collision and a seasick feeling at once. The toilet quivered under his thighs as the walls rattled and the front door—it must be the front door—cracked, splintering as though a tree had crashed through it, but there were no trees in the yard. He began to rise from the toilet into something awful, into a new sound, into the rising decibels of the woman screaming from the living room. Bent over, still reaching for his pants, he knew there would not be enough time to pull them up. He was aware of every facet of the bathroom then, as though he had been studying it for escape routes for months. The canary-yellow plastic curtain drawn halfway across the tub. The rusted showerhead releasing its slow, incurable drip. The colorless bath mat with its frayed, dirty edge folded up. The dingy rattan clothes hamper. The stale towel hanging from a nail in the door. And to his right, above the sink, a red hand towel limp on its clear plastic ring over the soap dish. The sink was set in a water-warped cabinet with a louvred door.

The frenzy in his ears stopped. Her scream was cut off. It had risen into a hysterical shriek and now vacated itself with a soft humph. Like a chainsaw dropped into a swamp. Chairs were falling, or maybe it was the kitchen table that someone smashed into the wall. Another tremor went through the house. No male voices. No commands, no shouting. All he had heard was a tumult and the hysterical clipped scream. The furniture dragging and feet moving.

He wasn't breathing anymore. He turned to his right, taking a step and holding his pants. He glanced from the faucet and the toothbrushes blossoming, one orange and one blue, from their dirty glass on the sink, to the flecked mirror with the bare ceiling bulb glaring in it and he saw himself. In hyperclarity. Alien, still holding his pants at his knees in one hand. He crouched at the cabinet, let go of his pants, and opened the cabinet door. His hands were trembling so badly they barely functioned. A vague pandemonium in the house was approaching the bathroom door, and the chaos that had been general now focused like a mountainside of storm water channeling into a narrow arroyo. Supporting himself with his hands on the tile floor, he plunged his legs into the cabinet, over a stack of toilet rolls, knocking over a bottle of Cloralex and the box of Detergente Roma. The rest of him followed so quickly, it was as though the cabinet had sucked him inward, his knees jamming themselves up against the sink plumbing, his naked unwiped ass sliding over packets of rat poison, his upper back scraping the cabinet's side panel, his head wedged beneath the sink. With his fingers at its lower edge, he pulled closed the cabinet door just as the bathroom door banged open.

In slatted half-darkness, he put his left hand down onto the cabinet floor. It was wet. The Cloralex had spilled, and the fumes were burning his eyes. He closed them, aware of several bodies entering the bathroom, saying nothing, creepily silent. He no longer heard the woman. He didn't feel her breathing in the other room. He didn't feel her in the world anymore. Cramped in place with Cloralex, detergent stench, and damp rot in his nose, he froze. Outside the cabinet, he knew his shit in the toilet was stinking up the bathroom. There might have been a spot of it on the floor. The men must be staring at the cabinet. Where else was he going to be.

A set of bootsteps, slow but springy, crossed the threshold into the bathroom. They halted a few feet in front of the sink. Nothing. No sound. Outside the house, though, he could hear two trucks, their mufflers cut away, racing down Alameda. Then this last set of boots came forward, stopping inches from the cabinet. He squeezed his eyes and could visualize the man, whoever it was, looking at himself in the toothpaste-flecked mirror. But he was wrong. The man had squatted. The cabinet door opened quickly.

He didn't breathe, he didn't move. Although he had been looking at nothing before, now he was aware of the knees and torso of a hunkered man whose jeans rose above the white-rooster stitching of his black boots. He was sure he hadn't even shifted his head, but his eyes must have opened on their own. He was looking at the strangest thing he would see for the brief remainder of his life.

The man squatting before him had an enraged, flushed expression, and his face, his whole head, was bobbing in the weirdest way, uncontrollably, like an ornament on the hood of a car going over bad road. The head-bobbing man's mouth opened and he hissed something in English, asking something, but it didn't make any sense.

"So you a Redskins fan, huh?"

*two*

## The Departure

Perturbed by a bird-punctured cicada
clattering in circles on the driveway,
he came into the house feeling ill. Paused
outside the door to the boy's room
where propped against the headboard
the woman was falling asleep
improvising a story for the boy
before his nap. Her last smudged words
and then a silence into which the boy asked
What then? What happened then? Standing there
behind the jamb, the intruder
holding his breath. Gone from himself
to let them go on.

*Marfa, Texas*

Until recently, people had always guessed Hoa was younger than her actual age. But at a Christmas party in Asheville, Dale overheard a friend say, "Looks like she's lived through something." That was six months ago, not long after what happened with their son. The stress had continued to work through both of them. Fingers through dough. Every morning, the bathroom mirror showed the lines deepening from the wings of his nose down to a place just wide of his mouth, and the furrow, like a chisel mark, set at an angle above the bridge of his nose. It was only when he overheard that remark about his wife at the Christmas party that he realized the extent to which grief and worry had etched Hoa's face too. From that awful day last October when their son landed in the hospital, Hoa had let her hair go natural, a shoulder-length horsey black, streaked with gray. Dale noticed, of course, but it occurred to him that he saw her differently than other people did: more as a composite of those faces that, for almost half his life now, he had argued with, kissed, and listened to—as when, for instance, she sat on the couch in the mornings and told him, in what sometimes seemed unbearably real time, her dreams.

She had nicotine-brown eyes, full lips, and a long, straight nose.

"A nose like a knife," wrote Rabelais in *Gargantua and Pantagruel*, the book Dale had been trying to read at the UNC Asheville library the afternoon he met Hoa some twenty years ago. He was a first-year history professor doing research that led him to Rabelais, whom he'd never read. In that moment, Hoa bent toward him to ask in a stage whisper if he knew how to turn on the lights in the stack next to his carrel—for some reason, the only switch to that stack was on the far side—and the knife analogy floated up from the page, attaching itself in Dale's mind to this student he didn't know. To Hoa.

It wasn't a particularly striking analogy, "a nose like a knife," but Dale had been mulling the merits of that translation of the French *le nez pointu*. He'd never studied French. Even now, twenty years after first meeting Hoa in the library, he couldn't pronounce a single word correctly, or so it seemed on their recent trip to Paris. At the moment she bent toward him with her question, he had been comparing two translations to see which he might want to read in English: one translator translated *nez pointu* as "snub nose" and another as "nose like a knife." Hoa, waiting to see whether he knew how to turn on the lights in the stack, definitely had a nose like a knife, thanks, he would learn later, to her American father. She also had, still leaning toward him in a stained white V-neck T-shirt, a shapely body and expressive gleaming eyes. She smelled like mulch. Dale stood up to show her the timing switch, and they started talking. She said she was just about to graduate and asked if he wanted to see her ceramic work in the senior exhibition. He was so focused on her lips—they were vermilion at their edges, the sharp vertical groove in her upper lip completely hypnotized him—that she had to ask him twice. With her relaxed confidence, her straight-shooter way of talking—giving her real opinion without worrying about what anyone might want her to say—with her sultry looks and her animate face—the way her mouth opened when she laughed, those lips, Jesus—she commenced a serious swerve in his attention. Aside from herbal eye-definer, she used no make-up back then and none now, twenty years later.

Until their son's accident, sex with her had stayed good throughout their marriage. Although the hair of her pubis had thinned and her breasts now sloped, the changes in her body fascinated him, and he was acutely aware of the corresponding changes in his own. Despite it all and the painful intensities of raising Declan, their headstrong son, there was a marvelous intimacy to experiencing so much time together in so physical a way.

Now, Hoa was sitting up on him in their hotel bed. When she held her breasts in her fine, skinny fingers, her eyes half-closed, she was at once herself and every bit the fulfillment of his imagination's erotic longing. They had begun making love slowly and gently after what had been a long grief-induced abstinence, months of her brushing his hand away or him failing to adjust to the abruptly shifting rhythms of her body. Tonight even seemed, at first, a little too planned. First there was her decision to take this trip with Dale during his summer break. Then the long flight from Asheville to El Paso and the exhausting drive in their rental car from El Paso to Marfa, smack in the middle of the Chihuahua Desert, just a few miles from the Mexican border. They had checked in at El Paisano Hotel, where James Dean, Elizabeth Taylor, and Rock Hudson stayed while the movie *Giant* was filmed. They'd had a glass of wine at the hotel bar, steaks with plum sauce and more wine at Maiya's, the restaurant around the corner, and then a stroll after dinner to the bookstore a few blocks away. They had crossed the railroad tracks to the Presidio County Courthouse. It was too dark to find the pair of screech owls they heard calling each other. So, in the still early evening, hoping to heal themselves on this journey, desperate to return to the realm of normalcy after all they had been through with their son, they found themselves back in their hotel room. Through the open curtain, light from a streetlamp draped the foot of their poster bed.

Dale wanted to go slowly, but Hoa seemed to be pushing him faster, riding him when she was on top, riding him when she was beneath. It surprised him when she started to climax, her breath quickening, her torso lifting, sinking back into the bed, her thighs shuddering in spasms, low animal groans breaking loose from her throat. She was gasping dramatically, clutching at him as though in terror or anger, wrapping her arms and legs around him, crying out, shouting almost. Suddenly he realized that she was sobbing spasmodically, her face was soaking wet. She turned her eyes away from him into the pillow, slid away as he rolled to his hands and knees, her eye-liner smearing her cheeks. She was saying over and over, "I can't stop, I can't stop," and Dale didn't know what she meant at first: *can't stop climaxing, can't stop loving you,* and then as he drew toward her and tried to kiss her tears from her eyes, saying *my love, my love* softly, even as she thrashed away from him, Dale realized, ashamed of himself, that she simply meant that she couldn't stop sobbing, she couldn't stop worrying about their son, that this release simply manifested a relentless, ongoing pathos that had nothing to do with Dale.

For twenty minutes, they were silent and awake and side by side. Separate in their breathing. If he were James Dean, Dale thought, he'd be smoking a cigarette. Hoa rolled out of bed and began to dress. It was almost ten. The door to the room next to theirs opened and shut, and they heard voices and then a TV through the wall.

"Dale." She was putting on her blouse, once more in control of her breath. "You're not going to sleep are you?" A touch of mischievousness edged into her voice. Denial. They were not going to talk about what had just happened. She was pushing through it. His eyes were closed, but he could visualize the twist in her smile, her widening eyes. This is how it had been going for months. As though she were stalled, unable to get her life on track again.

The depression would slide its hands over Hoa's shoulders and shove her under its fathomless water for days at a time. Dale would find her incommunicable, lying on the couch surrounded by pillows and unread magazines. At night, she drank too much wine and took too many pills. Then something would click, and Hoa would manage to reach through the devastation to some kernel of resiliency. She breached the black water and made contact with Dale, with her ceramic work, with their friends. She would be laughing on the phone, losing track of time in her studio, or cooking up a fragrant spaghetti with Greek olives and loads of garlic. But the intervals between her obliterations and recoveries had become shorter these last weeks. Dale wasn't sure if that was good or not. The road trip was risky, he thought.

Their road trips had often taken them south in the summers, into heat, sweat, barbecue sauce, and homemade pies. He had mapped this excursion—part of his research on the turn-of-the-century writer Ambrose Bierce—to try to reconstruct the last journey Bierce took when, in 1913, he saddled up a horse, rode into Mexico to cover the Mexican Revolution, and simply disappeared, as all the scholars said, "without a trace." Hoa loved Mexico. They had traveled there before, collecting ceramics. She owned a set of plates from Puebla and two stunning black-and-white bowls by Maria Martinez, which she displayed on one of the shelves she had built along the wall of their living room.

Those long shelves held several pieces by other celebrated potters too, but for Dale, it was the row of little animals Declan made as a boy and half a dozen of Hoa's own pieces from a series she called Cambrian Explosions—abstract but suggestive of early life-forms—that lit up the room like glowing ingots. Hoa had shown fairly regularly in the last ten years in galleries around the country, which was hard for ceramic artists, often considered mere craftsmen, not "real" artists. Hoa had some sharp things to say about those sorts of distinctions, and Dale had heard about them more than a few times. What he knew was that people in her field admired her, and she'd volunteered to give up a week of work to come along with him. The trip from Asheville to El Paso to Sierra Mojada, Mexico, could be a time of healing and renewal for them.

"Sunday night, Marfa lights," he mumbled with pretend enthusiasm into the pillow Hoa placed over his face. He was comfortable where he was, in bed—except for the fact that he couldn't breathe through the pillow.

## Marfa Lights

From their hotel in Marfa, Dale drove the rental car east to the
viewing station on Mitchell Flat. There were some half-dozen cars
in the parking lot and kids ran around on the wooden walkway
that perimeterized the station house. Nothing else but desert in
every direction they turned. Flatness spotted with dark shrubs,
and in the distance, black mountains rising along the night's glassy
horizon. On the far side of the station house, there were platforms
and a few yards of sand before the fence line identified the extensive land as private property. A round man in a T-shirt and overalls
was eyeballing a telescope on a tripod, and Dale and Hoa stood
behind him looking over his shoulder into the sparse scrub in the
dark. There was a little dry lightning, a crumbly low tulip-black
thunder. The nearly full moon ducked through cloud.

"Catch anything?" Hoa asked the telescope man.

"Not yet," he answered, still fiddling with the viewfinder. "But
we just got here."

Hoa and Dale stepped from the viewing platform into the sand
and wandered out toward the barbed-wire fence. Behind them,
across the highway, a train whistle shrieked and shrieked again
more piercingly, until the engine was close enough to hear the

steely *cachunk cachunk* of the wheels on the track. Heading into Marfa from Alpine. Still coming, massively loud even at a distance, across the highway. Hoa turned toward it as she felt the ground begin to vibrate, and then the train was there, flashing and hammering past the station house, each car yanked even with her gaze and gone like a series of doors slamming shut one behind another, and by now, everyone who had been searching for the Marfa lights had turned around in place to watch the train juddering and roaring and vaniloquent. Hoa and Dale stood beside each other, mesmerized by the stroboscopic sequence of cars.

"Should have brought binoculars," Hoa said, turning back to the desert after the last car rattled away.

"If anyone spots something, you know we'll all be jockeying for position behind that guy's telescope," Dale said, dipping his chin in the man's direction.

"One theory," Hoa said, "is there's a lot of quartz in the sand around Marfa, and the sun expands the crystals in the daytime."

"Really?"

"So at night the crystals contract and give off an electrical charge."

"Hmmm," Dale acknowledged. Being a potter, she knew a lot about the composition of sand and clay, and she knew something about geology. He didn't want to argue with her, but then he couldn't help from asking, "Isn't most sand in the desert made of quartz?"

Hoa chewed on that.

"I read there's something similar near Sierra Mojada, not far from where we're going. I'll show you on the map. It's called Zona de Silencio, where supposedly the sand's so full of magnetite—maybe from an ancient meteor—that no radio, no satellite signals, nothing like that passes through. Compasses don't work. It all dies. And in the seventies—"

"Yeah, I remember seeing something about that," Dale interrupted a little too avidly. "In the seventies they found talking apes there. And ..." he took a second to improvise, "they were worshipping an ageless writer. Last name was Bierce or something?"

"You're thinking of that really bad movie called *Planet of the Professor Never Finishing his Book.*"

Dale blinked, staring out over the fence. There was a living, moving world out there in the desert, utterly invisible to him: forked tongues flicking for a taste of mammalian warmth, nacreous beetles approaching each other tentatively with spread pincers, pocket mice diving into holes, birds nestled in bunchgrass, sleeping with one eye open.

"I thought the Marfa lights were supposed to be car lights reflected from a highway somewhere over in that direction," he said.

Hoa was still following her own train of thought.

"Actually, there *really are* exotic species in the Zona de Silencio," she said as though he had suggested otherwise. "Some rare tortoise and cacti that don't grow anywhere else. In the seventies, there was a missile launched from White Sands, New Mexico, that went off-course and crashed there. That's what the book at the hotel says. Anyway, same reports of mysterious lights there, just like here."

Dale remembered something. "Did you ever hear people call car lights, when they hypnotize you, did you ever hear them called Lucifer lights?"

She gave him a look.

Dale liked to talk about words the way other people talked baseball or indie music or wine. It was a quality she appreciated because she herself had particular defaults in conversation. She had come to realize that she could talk about clay bodies, shino glazes, and wadding techniques at length, in the kind of detail that didn't necessarily fascinate everyone.

They were quiet for a few moments, but they could hear the clomping and chattering of people behind them. The slate sky was streaked with cloud, the moon still bright enough to damper the stars. It was breezeless but cool.

Dale stretched.

Hoa said, "It may take a lot of Bud Light to see the Marfa lights," and he said "I don't know" at the same instant.

There was something wonderful and contagious about the way she was tickled by her own jokes. Her laugh rocketed into a delicious squeak, the whites of her eyes gleamed, and her smile, her even teeth, charged her face with life. Maybe they really *were* on the road to recovery.

"Head back?" Dale asked.

Just then, Hoa's phone rang, and Dale could all but see her thought leap out of her mind like a text bubble: *Declan!* She fumbled with her purse and dug for her phone. Dale knew she was thinking, *Declan, it's Declan calling at last.*

She looked down at the screen and her face changed so dramatically, he could see it even in the dark. She clicked the phone to silent and stuffed it back into her purse. Dale started to raise his arm to her shoulder, but she was already turning toward the viewing station. On one side, a huddle of teenagers snickered, and on the other side, lit up by red footlights, the same children who had been playing tag earlier were whining to the big man behind the telescope that they were bored.

*One Awake One Asleep*

The hotel room was cool and Dale was dog-tired, but he couldn't fall asleep. Now *he* was wondering what their son was doing. What was Declan up to? Where was he? Dale turned on his side, watching Hoa through the half-gloom of their small room. In their poster bed, her face was turned away from him. He reached over and ran his fingertip behind her right ear, up and back and over that prong of cartilage. She liked to be massaged there. There and her eyebrows. She was the only person he'd ever met who liked to have her eyebrows massaged. He'd never asked her outright, but assumed it was a Vietnamese thing. He traced a gland in her neck that seemed swollen. She didn't wake, and after a few more strokes he stopped.

On her back now, Hoa slept with her arms folded behind her head, taking a few feathery, snoring breaths and then going quiet, her face nodding upward. Dale was growing accustomed to the dark, and he imagined for a few seconds that he could see her nostrils flaring and relaxing. In the combination of lamplight and moonlight from the window, Hoa's lips parted. Once, she moved her left hand down under the duvet, and when she brought it back again behind her head, it released the smallest cache of her musk into the dark. Her breath, a soft purr, came in delicate little snork-lings that altered in sets like waves.

She rolled to her side again, facing him, lifting herself just enough to pull the duvet, which had caught beneath her, over her head, and she disappeared under it. A while later, still awake, Dale watched her arm stretch out, shapely and dark, and fall across the white duvet. Her arm was crooked upward at the elbow so her hand was even with her face, which had also emerged, her thumb available for sucking—if she sucked her thumb, which she didn't. The pre-linguistic *urrmmmnn* she almost spoke might have been an acknowledgement of some kind. Or an oneiric murmur that all was as well as it could be, considering.

*Early Morning Run*

At 5:30 a.m., Dale was in El Paisano Hotel's courtyard warming up. A half hour before, just after waking, he'd slipped into the bathroom, not disturbing Hoa, filled his shaker with tap water, and opened a packet of vanilla whey protein. He shook it, drank it, and then, stepping back into the veneer of daylight edging the drawn curtains of the room, soundlessly dressed for his run.

In the hotel's courtyard, the coffee tables were empty. It was less than an hour after daybreak, and the air was already warmer than it had been last night at the viewing station. The courtyard fountain was surrounded by dead grass and made a bright, cheery splashing that would go unheard later in the day when the restaurant bustle and parking cars ratcheted the noise level up a few notches. From the courtyard, Dale looked up along the stucco wall for his room. Faint shadows slanted under wrought-iron balconies. The room was dark where Hoa went on sleeping.

While Dale stretched, two women in uniform—a few minutes apart from each other—hustled through the architrave into the courtyard, crossing the bleached tile patio, each at ease in her regular body, just before the job altered her voice, gestures, and rhythms into those of a hotel maid.

Dale rotated his neck and then squatted to the right to stretch out his left inner thigh, reversing his stance to stretch the other way. Supporting himself with one hand on a wrought-iron chair, he crooked his leg up from the knee, gripped the toe of his shoe, and felt the pull deep in his quad. He swiveled his torso over his hips in a slow, cautious circle, going easy so as not to provoke a crick in his back, then stood up straight with his legs apart, rolling his shoulders up toward his ears, rotating them forward, down, and back. The stretches were part of a familiar ritual and he performed them noting the temperature and humidity—not yet hot but dry—and the breeze: none in the courtyard. The big-top clouds in the already lapis sky weren't drifting anywhere. The pleasure he felt was anticipation, in part. A grafting of memories from many years of running onto this fresh occasion, a curiosity about the landscape and the path he had scouted out yesterday. But perhaps the pleasure was less emotional than physical. His lungs hungered for big drafts of air, the muscles in his legs were addicted to the ketone of morphine that strenuous exercise released. In the weeks after Declan's accident, he knew that his insistence on taking daily runs kept him from falling apart completely.

He put on his headphones and scrolled down the playlist, to DJ Krush with trumpeter Toshinori Kondo. Clipped the player to his shorts, tucking a loop of extra cord under the waistband, picked up his visor from the table, and adjusted it on his forehead. He pressed the start button on his watch and jogged out through the architrave into the street, turning right on West Texas and right again at the corner. On West Lincoln, he went left, leaving the sidewalk for the street and taking inventory of his moving parts.

His lower back was a bit stiff as usual. The twinge in his left knee that he'd noticed during his last run had moved to the center of the patella. He looked to see how his step was falling, could see himself coming down first on his heel. He shortened his stride and lifted his knees a little higher so the impact zone shifted forward to the balls of his feet.

Then he quickened his pace to match the drumbeat in his ears. He neared a high school and took a left toward a rec center and some railroad tracks. Just before the railroad crossing, Dale veered onto a dirt road paralleling the tracks. He could smell tar and oil in the air. The sun was behind him, throwing his thin, foreshortened shadow ahead and to his right. It was hot, but too dry to feel himself sweating profusely.

When Dale's watch beeped the first mile, he checked his time. He was leaving behind the last unplumbed, peeling houses at the edge of the town. Across the tracks to his left, he saw a rock wall marking the old part of the Marfa cemetery. He crossed the tracks near the cemetery on a graded pebble road, picking up the dirt road on the other side. For the rest of his outward run, there were fenced fields with cattle or scattered horses on his left, and beyond the fields, he saw Highway 90 with its occasional early-morning drivers in their pickup trucks. Both the highway and the dirt road were ruler-straight as far as the eye could see.

For the second mile, Dale kept his head up, trained on the middle distance, but he also tracked the ground before him, scanning for rocks, holes, and snakes. The tempo of his footfall doubled the backbeat of the music. Checking his step, he noticed his gait was neutral and he was coming down on the midsection of his soles. The sun was on his neck and, with an economy of gesture, he reached up to turn his visor backward to protect his nape. The dirt road, like every dirt road he ran in North Carolina, was a weedy hump between two tire track depressions. It was easier to run where the tires had pressed pebbles and stones into the dirt, but he sometimes crossed the hump when he saw pitted-out or stony stretches ahead. On either side, along the shoulders, were busy anthills and shallow bar ditches full of weeds.

A scattering of thoughts and images passed through him: the three of them—Hoa, Declan, and Dale—walking the side of a rural road in Asheville, and Declan—he must have been eight or nine then—slipping down the embankment to a creek, slowly, ankle-deep in brown water, sneaking up to an enormous bullfrog that surely saw him coming but didn't leap in time. Dale with his arm around Hoa, standing at the edge of the road watching. And Declan hooting in celebration and clamoring back up the embankment to show off the bullfrog before he let it go again. The fat green and brown frog looking a little glum and embarrassed maybe, and Declan beaming.

Then Dale remembered the time when he and Hoa had taken Declan and a gang of his friends to the lake for a birthday picnic. Dale had put on a hair-and-rubber monster mask and chased the boys up and down the lakeside paths, roaring and wheezing, swiped by branches, half blind inside the mask that reeked of sweat and toxic polymers. The boys screamed and ran in mock terror. And that night, scheming to scare him back, Declan hid a red plastic iguana under Dale's pillow and a rubber snake under the sheets on Hoa's side. When he and Hoa lay down, surprise surprise. But Declan was already asleep by then.

After the third mile, Dale turned around regretfully. For the last few minutes, he had been keeping his eyes fixed on a tethered surveillance aerostat floating like a white beluga whale several hundred feet over the desert a mile or so ahead. He would have liked to run closer to it, but as soon as he turned around the sun was in his face and he felt much hotter. He readjusted his visor to keep the overhead sun out of his eyes, his pace slackening. The desert had become a reflective surface and big waves of heat radiated upward from the path. The fence posts, the cacti, the occasional corrugated drainage pipes lying in intervals under the path, everything seemed to beam its heat at him. With the bottom of his shirt, Dale wiped the sweat from his brow. He squinted against the ground glare and tried to spit, but his saliva was too frothy. Wiping his wet mouth with the wet back of his hand, he figured the air was already hotter than his body temperature. Unadulterated dogbreath.

An image of Hoa in the motel in El Paso flashed in his mind. Pulling on her pants. Those defined dancer's hamstrings filling them out in back.

And then he was sucked completely into his run and not conscious of thinking about anything until the watch beeped and he glanced at his time. Otherwise, he *was* his running. His body abducted his mind. His pace had picked up in the fifth and sixth miles until, two blocks from the hotel, he pressed the stop button on his watch and started walking. He took off his headphones. They were soaking wet. He had no memory of the songs he'd heard after the third mile. For the large part of the last three miles, he had existed in a pure present. The songs playing through his headphones were converted into perfect caloric energy. When his body was in tune with his run, anything—a stumble, a song, a little rise forcing him to lean forward—could be metabolized into usable energy. The run became his mechanism for climbing out of himself.

As soon as he entered the air-conditioned hotel, he began to sweat in earnest and by the time he reached his room, he was liquid.

Hoa came out of the bathroom in a white towel, combing her shoulder-length hair.

"You know my mom always told me it wasn't good for the roots, combing my hair when it's wet. She told me it would make me go bald."

"That's why I don't comb my hair at all," Dale said, crouching on the floor to unlace his shoes.

"Yeah, but you're going bald anyway." Her back was to him, she was sitting down at the desk. "So you must have done it a lot as a child."

Dale shook his head. He stripped and went into the bathroom, shaved, and turned on the shower. For a long time, he stood in the cold water, letting it bring down his temperature. *Run long enough in the heat and your brain begins to cook.* Afterward, he stepped into the room and stood naked with one hand on each lower bedpost like he was preparing to take a whipping, and he leaned there absorbing the downdraft from the ceiling fan. His feet had left wet tracks on the tile floor. Sweat began to pour out of him again.

Hoa, now dressed and sitting up in bed, lifted her face from her book. She got up and went into the bathroom and came out with a dry towel. While he stood naked under the fan, she swabbed the nape of his neck and his shoulders and lower back with the towel. She swiped his inner thighs, bringing the towel down his calves. One and then the other.

"Turn around," she said.

He turned and she leaned forward to kiss him on the lips. He hadn't brushed his teeth yet, so his response was hesitant, his lips closed. She wiped the towel against his forehead and he shut his eyes, enjoying the soft cloth as it descended his chest, belly, thighs. Then he felt her finger on him and he opened his eyes. She was tracing a blue vein that stood out from where his torso met his hips on the left side.

"It's like a pour mark," she said. She was thinking about glazes.

*Marfa Cemetery*

"So when we get there, I'll tell you how Ambrose Bierce died in Marfa," Dale said, standing behind the red rental car and lifting their two duffel bags into the trunk.

"Why don't you tell me now?"

She wasn't into surprises.

He looked at his phone. 8:16 a.m. He ignored her question, stepping back through the wrought-iron gate into the open courtyard of the El Paisano Hotel. The tall fountain burbled above the wheat-colored, ant-riddled grass. He walked to the table where he and Hoa had eaten toast with marmalade and gone through two cups of coffee each. Their plates and silverware were gone, but there was the Morris biography of Ambrose Bierce that he'd left next to his coffee cup. Inside the book were photocopies of his driver's license, the rental car agreement and both his and Hoa's passports.

Hoa was sitting in the car with her legs out. He shut the trunk.

"It'll be more fun to stretch the stories out," he said, sliding behind the wheel. "Three theories of Bierce's death. So I'll tell them to you in the three places we're visiting in the next three days."

"More fun for who? You might as well tell me now," she said, closing the passenger door, reaching for her seatbelt. "Anything could happen."

* * *

"Isn't that it?" she asked a few minutes later. They were driving past a small green highway sign for Marfa Cemetery.

He swerved right onto the narrow highway shoulder and let a pickup behind them go by. He pulled a U-turn, drove back thirty yards, and turned into the Marfa cemetery.

"Should be a new part and an old part," he said, scanning ahead.

The morning clouds had mostly moved on. It was a clear, dry morning, and the sky was blue and giant. A few trees shaded the edges of the cemetery, but most of the terrain was baked red-ocher clay, bearing clumps of desert grass that had been recently weed-whacked. Dale parked at the end of the cemetery's new section, where the graves were well-kept, and they got out and wandered around, stepping across a low cinderblock retaining wall into the old part, where the names were all Mexican and many of the inscriptions were in Spanish. The sun was sawing at Dale's forehead. Beyond the north side of the cemetery, brown prairie stretched all the way to a horizon of dioritic mountains.

Dale looked over at Hoa. She had taken off her snap-brim fedora and set it on a low, mold-stained tombstone. With both hands, she was working her hair back into a ponytail, something she did sometimes to soothe herself. Like taking a cigarette break. She slipped the blue bungee from her wrist and pulled it tightly around her ponytail, doubling it and doubling it again to hold her hair away from her neck. Another one of those practiced, graceful moves that charmed Dale. She put the fedora on with the knot of hair inside it.

As they dawdled through the cemetery, Hoa noticed the hodge-podge of markers, as various as the people under them must have been. Wooden and iron crosses, vertical and flat stones, a clay urn mottled with green lichen. The markers were sun-bleached, weather-eaten, and broken, a few reduced to nothing but splinters.

30

Someone had made a cross by nailing a broken chair dowel into an old plank.

"Look," Hoa called, a little quaver in her voice.

Dale came over.

"It's only 1932," he said.

"Not the date. Look at the wood grain."

"Oh yeah," Dale said. "In the cement. From the wood forms they used."

"Concrete."

"What?"

"Not cement," Hoa said, her voice steadier. "Cement's just an ingredient in concrete. Like 10 percent of it."

"Right," Dale said. "I know that."

He was wiping dust and dead grass from a stone. Two plastic flowers poked up from the sand beside it.

Hoa tried reading the inscription. "FAYECO? EL 31 DE DECEMVRE DE 1915 DE 2, is that an 8? DE ED. SUS PADRES."

"Fayeco," Dale pronounced. "Died the 31st of December, age of 28."

He held back the part about the parents. Parents grieving their dead son. She didn't need to go there.

A mockingbird was singing at them. Hoa wiped sweat from her forehead, then cleaned her sunglasses with the lower edge of her blouse.

Dale went on. "December 1915. This guy was probably wounded in the battle at Ojinaga. Died incarcerated here in Marfa. So one of the theories," he went on, "is that Bierce is buried here in Marfa in an unmarked grave."

He took a photograph and slipped the phone back into his pocket. Hoa was walking away toward a stone flush against the ground.

"Everyone on this side is Mexican," she called.

"Just about."

"Then why would Ambrose Bierce be over here."

"Just a possibility. Want to hear how it goes?"

It was a redundant question, but her lack of response didn't deter him.

"So it's 1913, Bierce was in his seventies, right? At the peak of his fame. He'd been a journalist at the *Chronicle,* he'd published his Civil War stories, and his *Devil's Dictionary* was a hit. He was traveling the lecture circuit with this pretty secretary young enough to be his granddaughter."

"Yeah, yeah."

"And he's a serious drinker, remember, and the rumor is he's having an affair with the secretary. Her name's—"

"Something Christiansen."

"Right. Carrie. But Bierce needed action. He was looking for some inspiration, a kick in the ass in his old age. And along came Pancho Villa with the Mexican Revolution. By 1913, the war had been going on three years."

They had reached the far wall of the old cemetery, close to the railroad tracks. Now they turned around and looked back toward the rental car. The old cemetery was all hardened clay and crumbled markers and spare brown grass growing in clumps like armpit hair. The new section, where they'd parked, was full of plastic flowers and gleaming sandstone monuments, all the way to the scrim of cypress trees by the highway. Dale wiped his wet forehead with the back of his palm.

"Let's get back to the car," Hoa said, feeling sweat beads roll down her lower back. "Were you thinking you were going to find a headstone for Bierce that no one else had noticed?"

Dale was already thinking about something else.

"I want to make a quick trip to Ojinaga. It's only an hour from here, across the border. Then we'll come back, go east around Big Bend and south to Mexico through Piedras Negras. We'll spend tonight there. Tuesday we'll visit Icamole. And Wednesday, we make it to Sierra Mojada. Okay?"

Another redundant question.

Inside the car, the seats had been baking and the steering wheel was hot under Dale's palms. While he started the engine, Hoa fastened her seatbelt.

"I just wanted to see what was left of anyone who was buried here in Marfa after the Battle of Ojinaga. Bierce was probably there."

Hoa said, "He went down to Mexico to cover the Revolution? Hot damn!" She jerked in her seatbelt. "The buckle's scalding."

"Yeah. He rode a horse into Mexico at seventy-whatever years old, not speaking a word of Spanish, and he trotted around looking for Pancho Villa. Who didn't speak English. Like he was going to get an exclusive interview. Just check the maps for a second," Dale interrupted himself. "After we come back from Ojinaga, we go from Presidio to Lajitas, right? Then north around Big Bend to 90 east, right?"

"Lajitas." What was familiar about Lajitas? Hoa wondered, plucking Dale's sheaf of maps from the glove compartment. "Isn't that where Ted Kaczynski lived in a hole in the ground?"

"I don't recall," Dale said as Hoa foraged for the right map. "I know it's full of end-timers and survivalists. Hard-edged hippies. It's supposed to be one of the real—"

"Can't wait."

"So, we go straight through it."

He leaned toward her. She leaned toward him too, the pages in her hand, until their shoulders were touching. The air conditioner was full blast.

Dale pointed his finger above Big Bend. "At Marathon, we go southeast through Langtry— that's where Judge Roy Bean lived, guy who called himself 'The Law West of the Pecos.' Held court in his saloon."

Dale sat back. Through the windshield, he saw a crypt guarded by three green marble angels.

"Bean set up a legendary boxing match. On a little island in the river, when boxing was against Texas law."

"Wasn't there a TV show named for him?"

"Judge Roy Bean? I don't know. He pulled some wild shit. Like he's famous for acquitting an Irishman of murdering a Chinese coolie since—get this—he said homicide is defined as taking a man's life but he couldn't find any specific law in the book about killing a Chinaman."

Hoa glanced up from the map catching Dale's eyes straight-on and then she looked through the windshield at the three angels. They seemed to have a doleful message to tell.

A few minutes later, beyond the Marfa town limits, Dale was speeding. On the passenger side, Hoa took in the dirt roads crossing cow guards and paying out into the desert or curling away behind maroon hills. She looked over a big empty plain with bunch grass and giant yucca with stick bouquets of creamy flowers. Along a rise, there were four scraggly trees and three black cows, each under a separate tree, staring into the dry air. Under the fourth tree, a recumbent black cow held up its head, absorbed by *quien sabe*.

Hoa felt a lot like that these days, as if she didn't know what she was thinking about. As if she were caught in a drift current. "You know something?" she said. "Every bit of this desert is fenced off."

"That's Texas," Dale answered. "It's all private property in Texas. Last time I was out here, I met a man in the Marfa bookstore. He had a little two-seater Piper Cub, and he offered me a ride. The next day we flew over Solitario, that incredible blown-out volcano and I got a sense, up in the air, of the geology. You see waves of thick rock angled up, cut away, curving hundreds of miles into the horizon. And you see these enormous ranches with feudal houses and outbuildings, sitting way out in the middle of absolutely nothing."

*three*

*Her Awareness Of*

The chickadee's scratchy racket.

Flare of rosacea along the side of her nose.

A few dry leaves waving from the top of bare privet.

Her intolerable sclerotic routines.

Long rebukes of morning rain.

That sleep inside of which she is certain she is still awake.

The tidal waiting for something to change.

Biting back the same questions.

The faint glow along a fragment of sincere feeling in a
personality she thought had been extinguished.

## Death of Bierce in Marfa

Between steep plateaus, Dale and Hoa passed rises of layered and striated rock and pocketed canyons. Ahead, at the side of the road, an enormous purple-beaked buzzard took a few slow-motion running steps away from something dead, flapping its black serrated wings. And then it seemed to change its mind and folded its wings and turned to watch them from the shoulder with serene disinterest as they sped by.

"So you never did tell me. Why would Bierce be buried in Marfa with the Mexicans?"

"Ah," Dale answered, checking his speed and slowing down.

"So the very last letter Bierce mailed to his secretary, Carrie Christiansen, remember? It was mailed from Chihuahua City, Mexico, and he wrote, 'Expect next day to go to Ojinaga, partly by rail.'"

"Yeah?"

"When he says 'next day,' he means December 27th. Because the letter was posted December 26th. So Bierce was in Chihuahua City Christmastime in 1913. And so was Pancho Villa. Villa was there rounding up men to attack the Federales in Ojinaga. You'd expect Bierce would want to follow him looking for the action. And just a little later, the second week of January—now it's January 1914, right?—Villa and his army attacked Ojinaga. Completely overwhelmed the fort. All the surviving Federales, their cronies and their families were hauling ass across the river looking for sanctuary on the American side at Presidio, which was basically a U.S. army base back then. And the U.S. army was rounding them up as soon as they made it across the river. All the refugees got packed off to Marfa, the nearest town with a train depot and a telegraph office. With me?"

"And Bierce?"

"So there's a record of a U.S. mercenary who says he heard an old gringo was shot in the Battle of Ojinaga. And a customs agent in El Paso claims to have heard the same thing."

"Oh that's really reliable."

Dale turned his head toward Hoa and caught the play at the corners of her mouth. She had taken her off her running shoes and was sticking her sock feet up on the dashboard. With her sunglasses on, she was peering through her splayed feet as through a gun site. But her face was animated behind her sunglasses.

"No," Dale admitted, "you're right. Those aren't eyewitness accounts. But then, years later, in 1957, an American driving through Arizona picked up this old man. The old man said he served with the Federales and fought against Villa in 1913. Okay? Forty-four years earlier."

"How'd the History Channel miss this?"

"Listen, here's where it gets good. The old hitchhiker happened to mention he was in Ojinaga when Pancho Villa attacked. Said he was running to get away across the river when he noticed an injured gringo. Or maybe the gringo was sick, he wasn't sure. In any case, he remembered the gringo's first name was something like Ambrosia. At the moment, with Villa's men after him, the Mexican was thinking that if he crossed into the U.S. with a U.S. citizen, it was bound to go easier for him, so this guy, the Federale, loaded the old gringo into a two-wheeled cart, a wooden wheelbarrow basically, and half floated, half pushed him across the river.

"But on the other side, the U.S. army was inundated with refugees and they just swept up the moaning gringo and the Federale along with everyone else and escorted them all to Marfa for, as we say now, processing. By this time, the gringo was completely delirious. He had a boiling fever and was just about in a coma. Sure enough, when they reached Marfa, the gringo gasped his last and kicked the bucket. Since he didn't have identification, the U.S. soldiers had no choice but to bury him in the old Camp Marfa cemetery."

"Ambrosia," Hoa said, weighing the word with her lips and tongue.

"Eyewitness account. This corroborates Bierce's intended location according to his last letter. So that's Bierce's first death. Just after the battle of Ojinaga, which is where we're headed now. He was wounded in Ojinaga and buried in one of the unmarked graves we just walked over at Marfa."

"Wow, look!" Hoa pushed forward in her seat. "A roadrunner! What's that in its mouth?"

While they were working on the body in the dirt, he reached down for the head, which had taken a roll to the side. He plucked it up by its ropey black hair and noted the sand sticking to just one side of the face. He swung the head gingerly back and forth a couple times, like a signalman with a lantern, to spin the rest of the blood out. In his other hand, he held the man's Redskins T-shirt, which he had told the man to take off before they killed him.

The shirt and the head he carried over to the side of a blue metallic Dodge pickup, holding the head away from him. He planted it neck-down in the sand facing the others, who were busy chopping into pieces the body to which the head recently had been attached. He plucked a seven-inch abalone-handled pocketknife from the front pocket of his jeans and sat down in a half-slice of shade against the front wheel of the truck, his legs scissored open and the head between his knees. His own head, and the white cowboy hat on it, bobbed noticeably in time with his pulse. When he got agitated, as he'd been a while before, his condition—which the gringo doctor called *aortic regurgitation*, a leaky heart valve—made him feel sick. It was like having the worst case of hiccups imaginable, and his head would nod out of control. It freaked out people who weren't used to it, but that gave him a kind of power he knew how to use. They called him El Palomo, the cock-pigeon.

Now he was feeling calmer. He stuck his thumbnail into the blade notch, opening his knife, cupped the forehead, and pulled the head toward him. He made an incision at the top of the head, pressing the point of the blade until it met bone. Then he drew it down the back of the head to where the neck began, feeling the tip of the blade scoring the hard skull. He put down the knife on the shirt and, at the back of the neck where the hair was thickest, he jammed his thumbs into the incision and pried the thin flesh to the side. There wasn't much blood and only a few quick velcro-like sounds.

Picking up and laying down his knife several times, he gradually scraped away the tissue underneath the hair and, using his fingers, worked the flesh away from the back of the skull. It was easy enough work, clearing scalp from bone, until he reached the ear canals in their beds of fat. They were like little rubber hoses. These he severed one at a time at their bases, close to the skull, then he peeled the ears forward. The other men and the teenage boy were laughing about something. A plane whined across cloudless sky.

Peel a little and cut. Peel a little and cut. That's how he learned it. At last, the forehead turned inside out and revealed two bizarre eyes sunk deep into their sockets, their irises afloat on white jelly. He slowed down. He didn't want to ruin the eyelids. Between the left lid and the eyeball, he pressed his index finger and, with his other hand, he guided the knife slowly around the socket. Then he did the right eye. One inadvertent gash at the corner, that was his only mistake and it didn't matter much. The eyelashes and lids and eyebrows all slid forward with the skin, making a soft slurping sound.

When he came to the nose, he wasn't as sure how to go about it. With a deer, you just cut through the nose, because later, you glued a standard black plastic nose on. At first he tried scraping the skin from the nose cartilage with his fingernails, but he was afraid the skin was going to tear. He decided to cut into the cartilage at the tip to release the skin.

The red thing between his hands had stained his jeans at the insides of his thighs, despite that he'd been careful. His neck itched. He carefully put the mess down upright in the sand and wiped his hands on the Redskins shirt—white cotton with a red Indian face on the front. Now more red on the shirt. He spread it out again and put the head on top. He'd have to burn his jeans. But first he'd sleep. He needed sleep.

He reached up to scratch his neck and pinched at something foreign there, flicking it away. Near his left boot, he noticed an anthill, more ocher than the ground around it, and a few tiny turquoise beads, or chips from beads, at the edge of it. No ants wandered out into the sun at this time of day. The man considered the turquoise beads for a moment. A burial site, it could be he was sitting over a burial site.

A beetle scuttled near his boot between clumps of wiry tabosa grass and paused to take its bearing or perhaps it sensed something threatening, a boot heel rocking in the sand.

The teenager approached, regarded the messy situation, and changed his mind. El Palomo checked the tips of his fingers before he adjusted the brim of his hat. He carefully tugged the Redskins shirt with its gruesome consignment toward him and leaned back against the tire.

Behind the ear holes, there was a little fresh blood where he had nicked vessels running through membranes under the skin, but the whole skull was slimy with dark clots and a bland yellow suet around the jaw and mouth. El Palomo rolled the flesh forward over the face, turning it inside out until he could see more clearly where the lips connected in a ring of tissue around the teeth. There was sand on his fingers now. He took up his blade again and swiveled it around the lining close to the jaw. As he split the lips from the gum, the knife scraped hard against buried teeth and he flinched.

He took a slow breath and looked up away from the others and into the desert. A roadrunner was standing still about twenty-five feet away, looking sideways at him. He considered, for a moment, whether it might be a sign of some kind and whether it was good or bad. He started to stare it down and it dropped its gaze.

As the skin pulled away, the skull immediately began to dry out in the heat. The flesh, too, was blanching. El Palomo glanced around for a clean surface. With both hands, he gathered the whole piece of raw skin, completely separated now from the skull, and stood up. He spread the pelt out on top of the front tire under the wheel well, and then he brushed his hands together, wiping them on the shins of his ruined jeans. He slipped the toe of his right boot under what remained of the man's head, and with what looked to be a practiced soccer move, lifted and flung it with a quick, fluid motion toward the roadrunner, which suddenly wasn't there anymore. The kicked hunk of whatever it was, now that it no longer resembled a man's head, landed against the base of a mesquite twenty feet away.

The others had finished what they were doing and one of them glanced toward El Palomo. There were five of them altogether, and two lugged something in doubled black garbage bags to the bed of a crew-cab Silverado. They went back several times, returning with more bags. They closed the gate, a puff of dust rising into the dry air, and without speaking they got into the truck and drove off across the desert in the direction of La Esmeralda.

One of the men and the teenage boy were left behind, talking and smoking and looking tired at the back of El Palomo's truck. From six feet away, El Palomo, standing up again, could smell the older one's cologne. It made him nauseous. Looking down at the pelt, he noticed something on his right boot. He bent and wiped it away with a clean swath of the shirt. Then he wiped the tip of his right boot against the back of his left calf, polishing it against his jeans. His boots were clean, obsidian-black, with two white roosters stitched into the vamp.

"Casi listo," El Palomo said to no one in particular. He wiped his knife on the sleeve of the Redskins shirt with some diligence, and then he stretched his arms and twisted his torso one way, the other. He put his hands together behind his back like he was hand-cuffed and raised them as high as he could, which wasn't very high, and he turned and rolled his neck, listening to the vertebral joints pop. There were no clouds to ease the blaze of the sun, which was still approaching the meridian. He felt the burn on his shoulders through his shirt. The sky was indifferent, colorless. He examined his blade, wiped it once more against the shirt, then folded and pocketed it. He opened the passenger door. In the glove compart-ment, he felt past the .38 Super for the wooden haft of his sewing awl. He pulled out the awl and sat again in the sand, patient, at ease, dialed down. He adjusted the brim of his hat against the sun's pitch.

"Unos de los balones," he said quietly as though talking to himself.

The man and the boy smoking at the back of his truck flicked their cigarettes to the ground at the same time. The older one, with the wilting mustache, reached into the truck bed and selected one of the dozen new soccer balls flocked against the tailgate. He walked over and offered the ball with both hands to the man with the jerking head. Afterward, he went back and picked up his cig-arette from the sand. The teenager had been observing him side-wise, his own half of a cigarette still burning in the sand. He took a casual step away, turning his back on the older man, and took off his hat. He combed his hair with his fingers, set his hat back on, and touched his shirt pocket to check for his pack and lighter. When he glanced down, he noticed that his long-sleeved shirt had a few bloodstains on the cuffs and front. Facing away, he lit up, drew, and blew smoke.

El Palomo plastered the human skin over the soccer ball, stretch-

44

ing it smooth. He took his awl and punched carefully through an edge of the scalp, pressing the needle at an angle through the outer cover of the ball so that it emerged an inch from where it entered. He pinched a loop of thread loose from the threading post, holding it taut with the fingers of his left hand as he withdrew the needle from the hole. When he had punched another hole, he fed his loop of thread into the needle's eye. As he extracted the needle from the second hole, the first lockstitch pulled tight.

When at last he finished, El Palomo stood up grinning. Brilliant white teeth. He held the soccer ball out toward the other two. Only then did he notice that they must have taken their hats off when they were working because he could see their shirts and pants were spattered, but their hats were clean.

What the two sicarios regarded in El Palomo's hands was a man's face badly sewn around a soccer ball. It didn't much resemble the face of the man they had picked up a few hours earlier. The skin was pale and thin as parchment and the eyeholes gaped, one backed by a black square and the other by a white one. The nose hung with no shape to it and the mouth was just a dilated rictus. No one's mouth looks like that, the teenager thought.

"Muy guapo," snickered the other, releasing the smoke in his lungs. There was a tic firing in his cheek.

The one holding the soccer ball turned it around, the ball's face level with his own. The others waited.

"Creo que necesitas un corte de pelo," El Palomo said to the soccer ball.

The older man mimed a laugh, but no actual sound came from his mouth. The other looked down and toed his new cigarette into the dirt.

"Vamonos," said El Palomo. The bobbing of his own head had slowed, and the other two could see that he had chilled out. Both were wondering which of them would be given the responsibility of holding the fucking ball while El Palomo drove.

## Snake on the Road

Maybe forty minutes more, and then they would cross the border, Hoa figured. An alloyed glare from the sky and landscape radiated through all the windows of their car, and even with the air conditioning on, they found themselves, every ten minutes or so, tinkering with their visors, Dale mashing his against the side window and Hoa trying to wrestle hers lower than it wanted to go against the front windshield.

Dale kept relocating his browning left forearm so the sun wouldn't sear the same strip of flesh. Like turning a roast. He would flop the arm, forearm down, into his lap for a while and then pry it against the door under the armrest. Hoa had plugged her phone into the console port again. She was scrolling through music.

Mesas slowly yielded to corraded canyons, creosote bushes to piñons. The landscape was at once relentless and changeable, exhausting and seductive. To the left and right were tangles of cave-fenestrated peaks and crags. Beyond those were higher mountains, spreads of mesa, and wider canyons.

Under the car the pavement hummed hypnotically. The highway would be empty for miles, and then they would pass a pickup, or an eighteen-wheeler would whoosh past them in the opposite direction, leaving their rental car trembling in its wake. Pink talus piled up below vertical canyon walls. There was a shimmer of heat rising from everything, but it didn't seem to blur the clarity.

Dale couldn't help but picture himself climbing the bare mountains, exploring caves he glimpsed from the road. What would it be like living in such a landscape? You couldn't help but imagine dropping yourself off out there in the primeval wilderness as you drove past in your air-conditioned capsule of a twenty-first-century car. Did everyone have that same fantasy? Was there something intrinsic to the ego that it had to project itself into spaces from which human presence was missing, into a terrain so brutally indifferent to human beings that, but for the road, it managed to repel almost any trace of the world's most aggressive species?

Dale glanced over at Hoa. She had opened her book, her face stressed, lined around the mouth, and her lips chapped. She must have felt him looking because she raised her head, her eyes questioning. Dylan was croaking to them both. Dale caught her eyes and turned back to the road.

He wanted to ask her something to break the stillness. While he too often thought about what he was going to say before he said it, measuring out his response according to what he figured his interlocutor expected him to say, Hoa was completely unaffected and never beat around the bush. He liked the way she talked about ceramics, honestly and directly, without false modesty or pride. She figured if someone asked, they were interested. And that's how she was herself. She didn't ask questions just out of politeness.

"So," he started. "Do you ever think back on mistakes you made early on? I mean after you started to work with Ray? Your first firings?"

She finished the paragraph she was reading and then dog-eared the page, putting the book on the floor between her feet.

"I don't know," she said, giving it thought. "You know, I've probably come to know myself as a ceramic artist mostly through my mistakes. So maybe they aren't mistakes. I remember early on, I was shaping something on the wheel, and Ray told me that my strength was that I had a good sense of form. He said plenty of his students could throw. Or they had other techniques really worked out. But maybe because of my dance background or my reading, I saw things formally and that helped me. So he always encouraged that side of me instead of critiquing my coffee mug for being too heavy."

"That first cup I bought from you was heavy. I liked the heft of it."

"Yeah. Another student said about a thick cup I'd made that if I hit someone with it, they'd die instantly. And Ray happened to be there, and Ray handed me the cup and said, Why don't you try it on him?"

When Hoa finished what she had to say, she didn't ask Dale something in return. She looked out the side window. It occurred to her that people were wrong to call the desert monotonous or monochromatic. Most of it took on a lion-colored tinge, that was true, but there were variations in every outcrop—sandstone reds and basalt blues, creamy schist, and burned whites. Green shadings of candelaria, creosote, mesquite. Yellow exclamations of yucca blooms. She could look at it a long time without losing interest.

She glanced over at Dale again. His face was refocused on the road, alert behind his sunglasses. He knew she was observing him, she could tell. She caught the little tightening in his cheekbones and jaw that, over the years, she'd seen him perform innumerable times in the bathroom mirror. Pronouncing the angles of his face. She liked his face best when he wasn't self-conscious. It was softer then, and its enthusiasms were easier to read. That was one of his great gifts, his expressive enthusiasms. From the way his body moved, graced with a ridiculous masculine confidence, to the way his mind did, empathetically, intuitively, he was as alive as anyone she had ever met. Which drew others to him. And exhausted him. She had seen him sagging with the weight of other's needs. Students, colleagues, parents, friends. Not usually her own needs. But when their son was in the hospital, barely alive, Dale had somehow managed to carry her brokenness, staying positive for her sake, reminding her to eat, talking her down when she was losing her mind. Dale carried her the distance, for a month, until they were sure their son was going to live. Which is when he finally broke down. And by then, she was able to rise to his need.

Hoa had canceled everything, and Dale had taken an emergency leave for the rest of his semester, which was almost over anyway. They drove to Washington D.C., staying for the first week in a cheap hotel not far from the hospital. They called friends for help, for advice, for contacts. One friend, who was out of town for a while, offered them an apartment in Southeast. So they picked up the keys from a neighbor and moved in.

Every morning they would wake from drugged sleep, both of them depending on Ambien and Xanax. Hoa would shower while Dale picked up coffee and croissants from Peregrine Espresso. Or oatmeal from Curbside Cafe. They sat together on the living-room couch, surrounded by their friend's books and records, going over plans for the day, making lists of which doctors they were seeing, which they wanted to get appointments with, where they needed to fill out forms in case they could get their son transferred to a private hospital. At 9:30, they'd take a taxi and enter the glass doors of the hospital into the bustle of doctors and nurses and also of others who had nothing to do with them, whom Dale and Hoa saw but didn't see, who also came at the earliest possible time to visit their loved ones. Dale and Hoa showed the guard their passes, walking the sequence of corridors in order to take out their passes again for another guard at the elevator that lifted them up to the eighth floor. Declan was heavily medicated for the first week and mostly he slept. Hoa would stand at the bed staring at the movement under his eyelids. They were like minnows, she thought,

49

wiggling over sand, iridescent and fleshy and alive. But when he did come awake, Declan was alien, interior, angry.

They sat with him and they grilled his doctors. Sometimes, Declan slept the whole day. Sometimes they thought he pretended to sleep. When he talked to them, it was only because he wanted something. He wanted out of there, but the doctors weren't going to release him.

When Declan's life was no longer in danger, he was moved to a lock-down unit with certifiably crazy people and a Chinese doctor who kept telling Declan how successful he could be if he concentrated on being good, making good grades, and finding a good girlfriend, platitudes that enraged Declan so much that one morning he leaped up screaming and physically threatening the doctor. He was immediately restrained by three big guards, shoved face down onto the bed in his doorless room, and given an injection in his buttocks while he struggled. All this as Dale and Hoa watched helplessly from the hall. Wanting to take their son's side and get him clear of the madhouse, but scared out of their minds about his precarious state.

Dale contrived to project a positive attitude. He told Declan that they loved him, that they were there for him, that he could count on them. But Hoa broke down. She couldn't talk to her son without trembling uncontrollably. Then Declan would close his eyes and Hoa and Dale would step out of the room and take a walk outside and talk about how it had all gone.

In the evening, when visiting hours ended, they went to various forgettable restaurants near the hospital. A Mexican place where they ate often enough for the waiters to remember them. A sushi bar. They drank before and during dinner and didn't regret it then or afterward. Wine, tequila, sake. They needed the alcohol. They talked more about what the doctors had said. After dinner, they went back to the apartment and sat together until it was time to take their drugs. Dale went to the guest bedroom, and Hoa stayed in the living room with the light on, until she began to nod off on the floral Victorian couch. It was as though they had become radioactive, their skins so supersensitive, they couldn't lie near each other.

For a month, life was completely encapsulated in their routine. If elsewhere people read newspapers and went to their jobs, if friends met for dinner, if fathers walked their daughters to school, if lines formed in front of Abercrombie & Finch where two half-nude models stood at the entrance joking with each other and letting customers ogle them, if anything at all was happening apart from Dale and Hoa's desperation and their son's suffering, they didn't acknowledge it because it happened in another world than the one in which they existed.

* * *

On the desert highway, there was little traffic in either direction. They'd been trailing a white pickup for ten minutes or so when suddenly the pickup swerved sidewise into the breakdown lane and swerved back onto the highway again. Dale glimpsed the balling, writhing snake at the same instant. He glanced into the rearview mirror and must have made some low sound, because Hoa asked, "What?" with alarm in her face, peering ahead at the road, then back at him.

"What are you doing?"

Dale was slowing down, pulling over onto the apron. Hoa's book jostled in her hands as the tires bounced over pebbles and sand.

"That asshole just swerved to run over a snake."

Hoa tried turning around in her seat to look out the back window, but her seatbelt restrained her. "And—"

"It's still alive, I just want to kick it off the road."

"You're not. Are you serious? It's completely dangerous." She filled the small space of the car with her protest. They had a long way to go, it was risky backing up, the snake would die anyway, trucks were coming. Nevertheless, he was backing up in the breakdown lane. Dale couldn't see the snake, couldn't see it, and then there it was in the rearview mirror. No closer than it appeared. He backed as far to the side of the breakdown lane as he could, opened the door and said, "I'll be right back," looking again to make sure no cars or trucks were coming. He jumped out and edged around the back of the car, which beamed pure malevolent heat at him, stopping for a moment to mug through the back windshield at Hoa.

The snake wasn't moving anymore. It was a fat rattlesnake of some sort, not too large, maybe three feet or so, it was hard to tell, the way it was twisted up and the tail end was smashed and the snake seemed to be dead. Dale was wary of getting too close. He stood a couple feet away looking at it. Beautiful simplicity. The face with its dark band across the eyes, the perfect geometry— oh, he thought, a diamondback—the big white scales underneath bloodied and black, annealed to the road. He considered for a second pulling off the inch-and-a-half long rattle and bringing it to the car, but Hoa would have a fit, and besides that, he didn't want to desecrate the snake that way. Dismembering it. A truck really was coming now. Flushed with the heat whelming from the road, he jogged back to the car.

The eighteen-wheeler whooshed by and the idling rental car quivered in its wake, the backdraft sucking at Dale's shirt and riffling his hair over his forehead. He opened the driver's side door, and they were on the road again.

"I've heard even a dead snake can bite you," she said.

"I don't think that's true."

"Heard it from a guy I dated once. He knew. He was a herp. That's what reptile specialists call themselves. He was my TA in biology.

He told me people in North Carolina are five times more likely to be bit by a poisonous snake than in anywhere else in the U.S."

"He told you that?"

There was an insistent *ding ding ding ding.* Hoa reached for her seatbelt and fastened it.

"I can't remember all of it," she said. "He'd been bitten twice. Once on the finger by a baby rattlesnake. It was just a nick, but he said it was like someone holding a match to his finger for hours. His whole arm swelled up and the finger turned black and he went back to the bar."

"Back to what?"

"He was from Onslow County. I think he used to go to a bar in the hills in the summer, and on the way he'd stop when it was night and brush rattlesnakes off the road so they wouldn't get run over. He loved them the way people love cats or dogs. I remember he said whenever the weather changed, he could feel the place where the bite-hole was in his finger. But the story I remember better was the other time he was bit. The snake wasn't even poisonous. He'd been showing me this fantastically long snake in his lab, maybe eight feet. It was skinny, not like a rattlesnake, a coachwhip. I asked him how he caught it, and he said he and his crew, the herps, right? — they were driving around near some new housing development outside of Asheville when he saw it cross the road. With all his crew looking on, he thought he'd impress them with some technique for catching snakes he'd read about in a reptile book he had as a kid. All this guy thought about was snakes. Knew everything about them."

"Except how not to get bit."

"He let me feed a cottontail to this diamondback in his lab. It was good enough for one date."

Dale adjusted his sunglasses. They were slipping down his nose on the film of sweat he'd exuded after stepping out of the car for forty seconds. Hoa had lifted herself using a yoga move and crossed her legs beneath her, turning in her seat so that her spine was almost against the door and she was facing him.

Dale glanced over at her. Her shorts had risen to expose that long, ribbony muscle in each of her inner thighs. Sartorius, the longest muscle in the body. Hers were amazingly well-developed. She still had a dancer's legs.

"So," Dale said.

"So he grabs this long coachwhip snake by the tail and straddles it so his back is to the snake. It's still trying to crawl away of course. And he starts yanking the snake forward between his closed legs. He told me the idea was to pull it through your legs smoothly so the head gets pinned behind your calves. Then you just reach back and grab it by the neck. It can't do anything to you."

"Yeah," Dale said. "I grew up doing that all the time. Me and my herp crew."

"But this snake was so long that before he could get enough of it through his legs to reach back for the head, it was swinging around."

"Like a whip?"

"Yeah, like a whip behind him and biting him over and over on his shoulders and his scalp. He said the worst part was looking over and seeing his friends in the car laughing their heads off."

"Sounds like a bright guy."

"Unlike my husband who stops to ferry dead snakes across the two-lane."

"Well," Dale said. "You have been consistent."

*Coming into Shafter*

Further on, they were driving past an immense horseshoe canyon, its scalloped vertical sides plunging down to a high talus slope dotted with bushes. Two golden eagles wheeled above the rim. Hoa thought she spotted a mountain goat moving laterally across the sheer red rock. She saw something, but she wasn't sure, and then it was behind her. Two tiny diesel buses swelled in the watery distance of the perfectly straight highway and roared toward them in tandem in the opposite lane. They had a brief glimpse of the passengers' faces looking through tinted glass at their own faces looking back at them, everyone imagining a fragment of a story for the other.

"Check that out," Hoa said, turning over her book in her lap, pointing to the mottled ruins of a building beside the road. In dense, blue-green brush a few hundred yards away, Dale could make out a rough circle of stacked stone columns.

"Maybe an old spring house?" Dale offered. "Shafter's up ahead. It's a ghost town, an old mining town. Last time I came, a few families still lived there. There's a little creek where it's suddenly lush, and a clump of trees full of birds. The bird noise was incredible. But mostly it's ruins, a bunch of old stone walls marked up with graffiti. And this cemetery where the graves are piled knee-high with stones. In the shape of caskets. I think it's to keep coyotes from digging them up."

Hoa said. "I'm low. Tell me something. It can't have anything to do with Ambrose Bierce."

"Alright. Turn the music down."

She picked her phone from the cup holder and paused the music.

Dale adjusted his sunglasses again so the pads wouldn't leave those indentations on his nose that he'd noticed in the mirror last night.

"Here's one I never told you. So …"

Hoa adjusted her seat back two notches, feeling more comfortable immediately. For as long as she could remember, all Dale's stories started with "So."

Dale smiled to himself, scanning for the right details before he started.

"When I was in school in Williamsburg, Brady told us he'd heard of some naturally occurring forms of lysergic acid."

"Yeah," Hoa said, already more animated. "I remember reading about that."

"Connected to witch burning in Europe, right?"

"It was like 60,000 people." She had a good memory for round numbers.

"They think it was connected to hallucinations people had after eating bread contaminated with lysergic wheat fungus," Dale said. "Hey, how do you know stuff like that?"

"Wait," Hoa said. "I remember. It was Andrea Dworkin. She wrote about witch burnings. She said the most common accusation—did you know this?—was that men claimed the witches made their penis shrink? That's what most of the women were burned for."

Dale turned his face back to the highway. A long stretch of straight road and rocky hills far ahead on the left.

"Hawk," Hoa said.

Dale couldn't see it, the sun was everywhere. He raised the visor and searched through the tinted upper band of the windshield, and then he saw the hawk, a tiny cross idling in dry blue air.

"Halcón. That's hawk in Spanish. It's what drug dealers call their lookouts, their eyes on the streets. Halcónes."

"So," she said, trying to make her voice sound like his, starting a story.

Dale readjusted the visor and re-tracked.

"So Brady ordered a bunch of Hawaiian Baby Woodrose seeds from *High Times* magazine. And we followed the directions, which I remember were phrased carefully in pseudo-historical terms."

"Meaning what?"

"Meaning it said something like: Although it's illegal to sell these seeds for the purpose of ingesting them, blah-blah, they've been used in Hawaii and in India for centuries as part of spiritual rituals. And traditionally they're prepared by scraping off the fuzz and grinding them into a paste that can be mixed with ... in our case, peanut butter."

"And it tastes like?"

"Unbelievably horrible. The directions said eat six of them, but Brady heard we needed to eat ten or twelve. Which is what we did."

"Smart."

"And within an hour, everyone but me puked, and I was worried I was supposed to puke. To get the poison out. But I couldn't."

"Everyone being ... ?"

"Just Brady and Mike and me. But it had a lasting effect on us, that night."

He glanced her way. Her feet were crossed under her, and she was looking out the side window. Her black hair was gathered up

57

and knotted with the bungee. He wondered how that could be comfortable when her head was against the headrest.

"It sounds corny, but I saw myself that night more nakedly than I ever had before. Or want to again. With brutal honesty. It was completely humbling. I'll never forget it."

This time she turned to look at him, but he was staring straight ahead and his sunglasses hid his eyes. She didn't feel like talking, but to restart him she asked, "Ever do it again?"

"This started out in Brady's dorm room, with candles and him playing guitar, and I began to have the sense that I knew exactly what Mike and Brady were going to say before they said anything. All three of us felt as though our minds had linked up. Mike would start to say something and then break into a huge grin because he could see that we already knew. It sounds bogus, but it was very, very real. We were communicating by intuition."

Hoa registered a shift in Dale's voice. Some diminishment of his presence as he excavated the memory.

"We had tickets for a Neil Young concert that night. On campus, so we didn't have to drive. And I remember standing in line outside the auditorium, and the moon was leaping around in the sky. I ran into a friend from high school and I couldn't talk to him. But I felt special, protected with Brady and Mike in this deep soft pocket of friendship and love. I was clear from any obligations and open to the world. Almost unbearably tender and receptive.

"And Neil Young came onstage singing 'Like a Hurricane' with monstrous industrial fans blowing out into the audience. A big wind *inside* the auditorium. From where we were sitting, it looked like the music was playing *him*. What those industrial fans did to the music, it was like the sound was coming from all around him, channeling *into* his guitar through his fingers. His skinny frame up there dancing around at the edge of the stage like a puppet hooked to a celestial current. And we felt it humming through us too."

Hoa took off her sunglasses to check the actual color of the landscape. The hills had gone from ocher to almost pomegranate. It wasn't the angle of the sun—it was still before noon. It was the rock, a different kind of rock, she decided. The geology was changing.

"Sometime later that night, after the concert ended or after we left, I ended up with Brady early in the morning on Dog Street near the Wren Chapel. There was something he wanted to show me, he said. And I trusted him. Everything, every word was brimming with meaning, every gesture a symbol, an omen, a promise. It was like we were beyond ourselves watching ourselves in a play in this parallel sphere.

"Brady showed me an iron manhole cover in the grass near the old stone wall and he said we had to lift it aside. There was just a finger hole and it was heavy, but once I lifted it a little, he got both his hands under the rim—perfect faith—and we slid the circle to the side and let her drop. In the hole, which was deep, maybe twenty feet to the bottom, there were these big horizontal pipes and a skeletal ladder next to a lit bulb on the wall.

"Brady climbed down and I was right after him. We were in a dark, narrow concrete corridor hung with sweating steam pipes, and everything—the walls, the floor, the air—everything was moist with condensed steam. It was like crawling through a cow—there was something maternal and uterine and nostalgic about the temperature and the moisture and the dim light. Along the corridor, there were light bulbs in metal cages about every twenty-five feet. Brady led the way and I didn't ask if he'd done this before or who with. We were beyond words in a mutuality of movement and thought and love for each other, in what felt like an eternal rolling moment."

Hoa liked it when Dale talked like this. She listened, scanning the road. There was a dark-green road sign ahead, but it was hard to read through the vaporous glare from the hood.

"We were walking along underground, parallel, I figured, to the stone wall in the courtyard, which meant when we took a right turn, we were headed for the Wren Chapel. The air was dark and breathy, like when you're sick as a child and your mom puts a humidifier next to you and rubs your chest with Vicks."

"Wrong culture," Hoa said, yanking Dale out of his reverie. "My mom did *gua sha*, remember? She'd oil my back and scrape it down with a spoon."

"The time you did that to me, I had a rash for days."

"You felt better right away, didn't you? So what happened in the steam tunnel?"

"So. We were mostly just walking through. I can't remember if we were talking or not. It was exhilarating but holy-minded too. I think we were quiet. We walked along a few minutes and then Brady kneeled at a locked iron door in the concrete wall. Just knee high, like a doghouse door. When I was standing beside him, he showed me how the shackle on the lock had been sawed through and repositioned so the cut didn't show. He took it out of the ring brackets and pulled the door open. I remember him hooking the lock back in the bracket on the selvage. I was thinking how careful, how really perfect his gestures were. And then he crawled through the opening, and I squatted down and followed him, pulling the gate closed behind me.

"We were crawling up a low-ceilinged ramp between two mounds of dirt in this brick chamber. The air was suddenly completely different than it was in the steam tunnels. I don't know how the change could come so quickly, but it was dry, really dry. I was sucking dust in Brady's wake and my throat was coated and the back of my tongue. It was like we crawled out of a soup bowl into absolute bone-dry permanence. I couldn't see well, but I could tell we were inside a vault about the size of a van, too low for us to stand up all the way. I could hear Brady striking a match and then I caught a quick flash of two brick crypts in front of us. And I could see there was no door, no other way in or out. Then the flare shrunk into a small steady flame that blinked out after a few more seconds and we both stood up hunched over.

"When Brady talked, his voice sounded weird and shaky. I knew it was the drugs, but I was spooked anyway. He said he thought this was Lord Botetourt's tomb maybe. And he struck another match. All my energy was draining out as if I were caught in an undertow. I fought against it enough to step up to the crypt when Brady lit a third match. I was looking for markings, I tried to see inside, I didn't quite know what I was doing. I didn't see anything particular. There wasn't any particularity anymore. And I realized that in the steam tunnel, there had been the noise of steam in the pipes and the echo of our steps and our breathing and here there was no sound. No moisture, no sound, no light, no air, no life. Brady was completely mute and I couldn't hear him thinking anymore. I was sure his thoughts and mine had been obliterated by—by the close presence of death. Which is no presence at all. A vacuum. It sucked at us so hard, we couldn't leave.

"I remember both of us sitting there, about six or eight feet between us, swallowing up the defunct air, the superfine dust contaminated by death, while it ate into our vitality. I'd heard about bad trips, and I was vaguely conscious of trying to modulate the feeling inside me to keep from going blacker, but I couldn't. I was alone with death. And Brady too. And death had nothing at all redemptive. No sense of being part of a cycle. Or a process. Or the mother of beauty, any of that. It was the end. It went nowhere. The dusty air smelled like our lives blown out, and the smell was all over us."

For a while, Hoa didn't say anything. They were passing an old house in disrepair on the side of the road, its adobe weathered away to reveal clods of clay. The concrete lintel above the door was exposed too, and thin wooden spouts extended from the parapet—maybe a water line had been roughed in, she wasn't sure. Then it was behind them, and she wondered who had lived there and what happened to them. She didn't like it when Dale talked about death.

Dale took a deep breath, drawing himself out of his story back into the sun-bleached present where he adjusted the bridge of his sunglasses. Where did he think he was going with that, anyway? That was the wrong tale to tell. Like she really needed to hear something bleak. Idiot.

Hoa looked out the side window. She asked the desert if she would ever feel normal again. Would she start to get some traction in her life?

"How's the gas," she asked, still facing away from him.

"We're okay."

"You want me to drive?"

Dale thought about Hoa's driving. She would doggedly commit herself to the slow lane, following the slowest of the slow cars with no impulse to pass even if she were going forty in a sixty-five zone. Just the same, he wouldn't mind taking a break. He could make some better conversation and maybe read to her a little from *Alone in Bad Company,* the Morris biography of Bierce.

"Maybe next stop," he answered.

"You ever take those seeds again?"

A bird flying fast and low from Hoa's side slammed the middle of the windshield. Dale hit the brakes and simultaneously checked his rearview mirror. A truck about half a mile behind him.

"What was it?" Dale asked.

Hoa's crossed sock feet came out from under her and she sat forward in her seat, the seatbelt jerking taut across her. On the windshield she could see two white marks the size of quarters where the bird's breast had exploded.

Dale slowed after the impact, but now he was accelerating again.

"It was a whip-poor-will," she said, the image frozen and precise in her mind, as though the impact had lasted a whole minute.

"It was a whip-poor-will," she repeated. "They usually aren't even out in the daytime."

"Don't take it as a sign," Dale said.

* * *

Two weeks earlier, Hoa had asked Dale, "Do you want me to come with you? On your trip?" Dale was on his way to the kitchen to fill up his thermos with coffee and drive to the university. He turned back toward her.

"Sure," he said. "If you want to." He thought about what that might be like. "I'm just afraid you'd be bored. I'm going to be packing a lot of research into a few days. It wouldn't be exactly like a vacation for you."

"You didn't invite me," Hoa said. "It's alright if you want to go alone."

Sitting on the couch in her Drive-By Truckers T-shirt and dark-blue stretch pants, her novel on her lap, she looked pouty. He could tell she was trying to read his body language where he stood in the doorway.

"I'd love to have you come if you want to," he said, squaring up. "I hadn't thought about it because it's just going to be driving around in the desert. And it's summer, so it'll be stupendously hot. I'll just be poking into these towns where Ambrose Bierce went or where someone claimed to have seen him."

"I'd be game," she said. She squeezed the contact from her left eye, placing it on the tip of her tongue to clean it, then balanced it on her forefinger and put it back in her eye. It always unnerved Dale when she did that.

"It's not the Mexico you like," he said.

"It's not the Mexico I've been to before," she answered.

Her cellphone rang from her purse and she bent over to dig it out, checking the caller ID. She dropped the phone back in her purse, still ringing, and resumed her position. There was a stack of books on the floor by her purse. Dale was a reader, but Hoa out-read him about three to one: novels, science, field guides, poetry, art books. Most of the best books he'd read over the years — aside from what he read as part of his job — were her suggestions.

Dale took a step into the living room. On a table, under the reading lamp, there was a photograph of all of them: Hoa, Dale, and Declan at about eight years old, taken in front of a cracked concrete wall in Cancun. The ocean was in the background, an unreal turquoise.

"Well," he said, "come then. I'd love the company."

She looked down at her novel, saying, "I could help you identify plants and birds and things. We might come across some ceramics."

"Yeah," he said. "I'm not sure how useful that'll be for an Ambrose Bierce book, but you'd make it more interesting for me."

"Definitely would," she said. She pushed her book forward, then she stretched out on the couch on her stomach, her legs behind her bent up at the knees, her feet waving in the air.

He took another step toward the couch, deciding. She was eyeing her open page again and her legs were wagging slowly back and forth, her pants tight across her butt. Now she was looking up at him again.

"Yeah, come then. As long as you're not going to be bored."

"I love Mexico," Hoa said. Her phone had stopped ringing in her purse on the floor, but now it beeped, letting her know the caller left a message.

"Okay, we're on."

It would be nice to be together in Mexico, he thought. What worried him was that they wouldn't be there on equal terms. He had to get home to do the writing and also prepare for the next school term. There wouldn't be much time to take the kind of side trips she would want to take. He'd end up in charge: his trip, his schedule, his research. He'd have to be careful about that.

"Are you sure?" Hoa asked.

"Sure. Vamonos."

She looked back at her book. Her feet still waving lackadaisically back and forth over her butt.

"Let me think about it," she said.

*four*

*Equal to These Flowers*


Such moments he marks,
recalling them to his son—as when
they sledded Suicide Hill and spilled
from the sled, the boy landing on top
of his father who slid in his slick down
jacket down the hill on his back
clutching his son, the both of them
wheezing with laughter—
freeze into set pieces through the father's
reportage and are finally, for him, far
less affecting than what
goes unmeasured and floats
around him with motes
of dust. Ordinary and unsorted.

## Crossing the Border into Ojinaga

A little more than an hour after they left Marfa, twenty minutes after they passed Shafter, they drove into Presidio, Texas, through rocky hills spackled with white caliche, like toothpaste flecks on a mirror. Before crossing into Ojinaga, they stopped at the border-patrol station, going in to show their passports and pay for a vehicle permit and a tourist card.

On the Mexico side, there was the casual flow of pickups, their windows down, *norteño rancheras* blaring. Drivers greeted each other as they passed, mustachioed men wearing cowboy hats. The main street curved between blocks of faded, multicolored houses, little tiendas, and vacant lots toward the zócalo. Most of the cars were old, the trucks crusty and lopsided. And then, some flashy new GMCs or Ford Lobos with jacked suspensions and tinted windows and brassy corridos ay-yi-yi-ing inside.

It was late morning and the zócalo—a sunbaked, concrete promenade in the center of a sprawling, dusty town—was treeless. After finding a parking space along a side street, they rolled out into the blazing heat, standing next to their open doors, stretching. Dale bent to touch his toes and Hoa arched upward into the Salutation position, hearing her spine plunk like a cello string. No pain, just a dull D sharp. The light was dazzling as they strolled back to the zócalo on the shady side of the street. Sweat trickled below Dale's underarms. He felt creaky.

A tertulia of taxi drivers wearing white Texan hats sat playing cards under a flimsy wooden trellis in one of the few shady corners of the zócalo. At the head of the concrete promenade next to a little clock tower reading 10:12 gleamed a life-size statue of Benito Juárez. Facing the arches of the municipal building across the street, the former president of Mexico held one arm tentatively in front of him. Under the other arm, he was carrying a bronze book. Dale went closer to see if there was any lettering on the cover.

"It says something," he called to Hoa. But when he turned, he saw that she had already drifted away. He took out a folded paper from his back pants pocket—where he used to carry his wallet before someone told him it was terrible for his backbone—and he made a note: *Juárez statue. Leyes de Reforma. 1857.*

Coincidence, he thought. They'd been talking a while ago about Judge Roy Bean. Like Benito Juárez with his volume of legal reforms, Bean was famously associated with a book. The 1879 edition of the *Revised Statutes of Texas.* It was the single book the judge ever consulted, as he frequently boasted.

Dale held his hand over his eyes, surveying the plaza. There weren't many people out, no teenagers at the zócalo. On one side, there were some shops and a restaurant. Hoa had walked across the street over into the portico shade of the café-con-leche-colored municipal building. There, on either side of the entrance, Dale could make out a few men sitting on benches. A brown dog with hanging teats crossed the street toward Dale, paused to eye him nervously, and changed direction. Then Dale saw the two teenage soldiers, each with a machine gun slung over his shoulder. They were posted under the portico, staring into the bleached street.

Dale crossed, following Hoa. She had turned from the wide

porch and gone through the inner arch to the center patio of the municipal building. Inside, she was holding her fedora against her belly, her sunglasses hooked in the button of her blouse, and she was gazing up at an oversized mural painted across four walls. Dale sidled over, taking in the wrap-around mural. A few men and women were shuffling through various office doors around them and were visible on the second floor.

"Does that priest have fangs?" Hoa asked in a hushed voice, her eyes riveted to a black-cloaked figure.

Dale turned. "I don't know. Looks like a case of good priest, bad priest. Because the one over there in the other panel," he nodded, "I'm pretty sure that's Padre Hidalgo. Leading the people into revolution."

"Pretty rare to see a priest as a vampire in a country as Catholic as Mexico, isn't it?"

Dale wasn't sure. The one priest had some long incisors.

Stepping back outside, they began exploring the streets of Ojinaga. Hoa put on her fedora and Dale realized he'd left his visor at El Paisano Hotel in Marfa. The sun was more vicious here than in Marfa and it seemed directed at Dale's forehead once again. They followed narrow streets, trying to stay to the shadow side, but there was less and less shadow. A man behind a street-corner food stand was ladling out bowls of tripe soup. Near a dark little tienda where women were buying bags of white tortilla dough, Hoa and Dale were forced to step off the sidewalk as roofers heaved chunks of tile and wood in the general direction of a dumpster. Clouds of white dust drifted across the street.

"Did we just walk into a snow globe?" Hoa asked.

They held their breath until they covered half the block.

Now and again, a street would lead to a vantage point from which they could see a wide, cultivated valley that was greener than on the other of the border. The gray mountains of the U.S. glimmered.

Soon, the pavement gave way to dirt, and they were in a poorer neighborhood where the adobe was unpainted, falling away in slabs, exposing scalloped and pocked clay. Under flat roofs and patchworks of tarp, old women watched them from open doorways. Pariah dogs skulked or lay inert on the edge of the street. The air was rank with burning trash. A man on a listless burro clopped past, averting his eyes. Ahead looked like more of the same, so they turned back, keeping to the middle of the street.

Near the place they had parked, they stood pressed against the shade of a cantina next to a corn cart. The boiled corn was placed on the grill, the vendor squeezing lime juice on the roasted ear and pinching red chili onto it. It smelled fantastic, but Dale was wary about the water it was boiled in. Hoa was admiring the view into the valley as two boys on bicycles zoomed by them on the wrong side of the street, descending the hill, careening around the corner and out of sight.

"It was supposed to be impregnable, Ojinaga's fort, because it's built on this mesa," Dale said. "If Bierce was wounded here, he was probably inside the fort with the Federales."

Hoa looked down the hill after the boys and then out to the cultivated pasture with its stand of cottonwoods and scattering of thatched mud and wattle houses. She said, "They call it the Rio Bravo don't they?"

"More like Rio Trickle by the time it gets to Mexico."

A little further on, Dale stuck his head inside a farmacia, asking if it was open. It was, they just turned the lights off to keep it cooler. Dale stepped inside, Hoa after him, and he asked for directions to the old fort. After a brief discussion with the young female clerk, the elderly woman at the register called out *Luis, Luis,* until the pharmacist emerged from the back, curious and friendly in his white smock, carrying a green book with a painting of fruit on the cover.

Dale glanced down to make out the book's title. *Alimentación y* something *erapia.*

"Nada más que ruinas," the pharmacist said softly, regretful about disappointing them. He put his book down on a stack of other books.

"Pero ándenles, take a look." The pharmacist indicated the way with his arm, which made him briefly resemble the statue of Benito Juárez. "Two blocks right, two blocks left."

"Oh, una cosa más," Dale added. "Is there a hotel here called The Palace Hotel or an office called The Foreign Club, El Club para extranjeros?"

The pharmacist stared at the glass counter, pensively scratching his cheek with his index finger. He consulted the young clerk and they both spoke with the elderly woman behind the adding machine. No, no, they had heard of nothing called by those names.

"Thanks then," Hoa called. The cowbell above the door clanked again as they went out.

"This is great," Dale said, following the pharmacist's directions. "So during the Revolution, this fort, which was supposed to be impregnable—"

"Right."

"—and a customs house by the river went back and forth between Pancho Villa and the Federales about four times. At one point, there was a Scottish mercenary working for Villa who helped stage a fake attack. Villa was famous for mounting huge cavalry charges, so this mercenary stampeded a bunch of horses with branches and tin cans tied to their tails toward the customs house here. The Federales were dug in in foxholes—" Dale put his hand to his forehead, scanning, and pointed north, "—over that way. And from their foxholes, they heard this incredible racket coming toward them. They figured it was Villa and his army charging. So they panicked and fled. But Villa wasn't even in the state then. It was just this Scottish guy and a general of Villa's with a pack of horses and some stray detachment of troops."

They came straightaway to the old fort in the middle of town. It took up a full city block; its four outer walls had been painted yolk-yellow a long time ago. Around the footings, brick showed beneath adobe. Old wooden doors in the wall had been mortared up, but musket holes still gaped in the upper sections. Just enough of the ramparts remained to suggest that there had been crenelations.

They crossed the street to look into the fort through the main gate. Adjacent to the gate was a stand-alone sentry house not much larger than a sentry. Peering through the small window, Hoa exclaimed something in Vietnamese. Then, "Think of the hours those men logged in this tiny oven."

Bolted to the shattered timber of an old portcullis, chain-link fencing kept them from entering the fort, but they could see into the large courtyard and to the back wall, which was mostly rubbled.

"So Bierce would have come here before Villa's troops, presumably," Dale said, wanting to keep her interested in his detective work. "I think a lot of the garrison fled before Villa actually got here, especially women and children and the rich. The fight went on for several days."

"Do you think that's a barracks? Or a magazine?" Hoa pointed through the fencing, across the rubble, to a small stone building attached to the inner rampart. She answered her own question while Dale was thinking about it. "Maybe a guardhouse. It's got barred windows."

"Good eye," Dale nodded. "What if we walk around the other side?"

He thought he felt his phone vibrating against his thigh and pulled it out of his front pocket. It was turned off.

"You go ahead, I'm going to scout out a place for brunch." Hoa held her fedora between her knees and lifted her hair from the back of her neck. The fedora's sweatband had left a red indentation in her forehead. She put her bungee around her wrist and pulled her hair down over her shoulders.

She was good at finding places to eat and she had a talent Dale lacked for ordering the right thing from the menu. But remembering the soldiers, Dale said, "Why don't you come with me, just a couple minutes. I wrote down a place to eat already." He reached into his back pocket for his notepaper, unfolded it, and pretended to look for the name of a restaurant.

A car with someone calling through a loudspeaker in a raspy voice, missing almost all its human qualities, puttered slowly up the cross street.

"Something about a vote," Dale translated for her, still looking at his notes, trying to remember the name of the restaurant he'd seen near the zócalo.

They were standing at a corner beside the cart of a meat vendor, whose warm, fly-encrusted carcasses hung in the late-morning air from a rack over his block. A woman was buying something boneless that he had just chopped into four red sections, weighed on his scale, and slipped into a clear plastic bag. The bloody meat, the brass weights, and the woman's money all passed in brisk sequence through the butcher's thick fingers.

"Los Comales," Dale said, "that's the restaurant. It's what?"—he looked—"almost eleven, but they might be open already. We can trade dollars for pesos there."

The two boys on bicycles appeared again, pedaling slowly, directly ahead of them. As they turned the corner, first one and then the other turned his head toward them. Checking them out. Hoa glanced at Dale, but he hadn't noticed.

\* \* \*

After serving two tours in Vietnam doing clerical work on account of his flat feet and bad eyes, Hoa's father had become an accountant. He met Hue, Hoa's mother, in Hanoi, where she worked for the U.S. embassy. He married her and flew her to Charlotte, North Carolina, in 1967, where she eventually found work as a court reporter. Hoa was born in 1970. She was nine and an avid ballerina when her father died of a stroke, leaving her mother to raise her through some difficult teenage years, finally sending her to the University of North Carolina at Asheville where she graduated with a degree in art—useless according to her mother. Hoa met Dale, with his high Swedish cheekbones, his angular shoulders, and his runner's build—in the library. But their first real conversation took place at her senior exhibition, just before she graduated. Dale had circled back through the show to ogle a big shino-glazed vase that Hoa had fired. It was her first experiment rubbing her vases, still warm from the kiln, with iron oxide, which dramatized the crackly texture. Dale reintroduced himself, which was unnecessary—she certainly remembered him from the library—and they talked briefly. Hoa studied him as he walked away. He was a professor, and so, in some sense, off-limits, but she was just a few weeks short of no longer being a student. Six months later, after joining Studio Clay Co-op, she had another show, and she made sure to send Dale an invitation.

After that second show, Dale asked if he could come to her studio to see her work. She said yes before she realized that she didn't know whether he meant he wanted see her *at work* or see *more of her work*. Hoa had been making a series of what she called Cambrian Explosions. Soon, Dale was sitting on a stool at one end of her studio, watching her open a plastic bag and dump a thirty-pound block of clay on the table.

Hoa told him she didn't want to explain her work, that he would probably get a better feel for it by seeing the process than hearing her go on. She said she was going to try to forget Dale was there, that he could leave whenever he got bored. She started to put her headphones on, then looked up at Dale—all good posture and attentiveness on the stool—and she put them back on the table.

Dale watched her wire off a thin pancake of clay from the block and slap it against the studio wall. It stuck there, and she wired off another pancake, slapped it against the wall, and did the same thing, again and again until the block of clay was gone and the concrete wall was full of clay pancakes that she peeled off and slapped on the other way around.

"Doing this, it loses its extra moisture," she said without looking in Dale's direction. "We make the clay out back. I like a groggy clay body."

She plucked the pancakes from the wall and mixed and beat them together on the worktable, wire-wedging and paddling the whole thing.

"Gets the air bubbles out," she said to the clay.

Dale was noticing the definition in the muscles of Hoa's forearms.

She laid a canvas cloth on the table, then looked toward Dale. He seemed genuinely interested.

"I start on the table here where I can see the shape clearly," she explained, lifting the mass of beaten clay and slamming it down, stretching the clay into an oblong platter-like shape that was heavier at one end than the other. She rotated the clay and lifted it up to her chest. In her sleeveless black T-shirt, the toned contours between her biceps and triceps sharpened. Her muscles filled with blood and her skin began to glisten with exertion. As she worked in the small studio, she was serious and intense. The studio had two doorways, but no doors, a stool for him, an L-shaped work table with a potter's wheel, a rack of shelves full of ceramics, a scattering of tools, and that was it. Other potters were working in connected studios or in other areas of the warehouse. Dale couldn't look away. He might be the professor and she, recently a student, but it was clear to him that she was in no way intimidated. He was only seven years older in any case. It wasn't a big difference.

At the table, Hoa took up a couple tools and etched marks in the clay that, from where he was sitting, he couldn't make out. She laid out the canvas cloth on the floor between the worktable and Dale's stool, placing the clay on top. She straddled the canvas in her running shorts, bent, and lifted up the clay, thirty pounds worth. Twisting to the left and starting a rhythm in her midsection like a golfer, she swung it outward. Then, using that torque with her legs fixed in place, she swung the hunk of clay back—pure centrifugal force—her arms extended, her whole body rotating as she slammed the clay to the canvas between her legs. The clay made a sound like someone getting punched in the stomach, flattening into an oblong.

When she had lifted, turned, and slammed the clay several more times, she set it back on the worktable and asked if he wanted to see the next part close up. He was up off his stool and beside her in an instant.

The scratch marks and depressions she had made earlier with the tools had been stretched into long craters and curved bands. She used both hands to squeeze one edge of the clay upward into something that looked to Dale like a cobra head. She repeated the process on the other side.

"I want to give it more lift over here," she said looking Dale right between the eyes. "Make it eye-sweet." Then she put her hands under one side of the clay and it took on the quality of a wave.

Something's eye-sweet, Dale almost said. "You plan this all out beforehand?"

Hoa told him that she couldn't plan it. She'd recently developed this shape and she wanted to work with it for a while. But the shape was different every time she stretched it. She might make seven or eight works in an afternoon and keep only one of them. The others she would pound back into formless clay.

She showed him some of her finished pieces, and he picked one and bought his first ceramic sculpture. Two months later, he had three ceramic sculptures and a set of tableware and cups. She had a note from him that she kept with his other notes in her sketchbook.

*I'm eating lunch, meeting people, planning lectures, getting a coffee, and what's really happening is a riot inside me. A riot of you inside me. Like all spring's flowers are thrusting up at once and the crust of the earth is crumbling and sliding away to make room for such color.*

Don't fall in love with this guy, she thought. You're too young. That was October, just before the first time they slept together. He sent her several letters in January, during his semester break, when he and his sister were moving their mother into a nursing home in Virginia. He said he wanted his life to fly into hers.

In February, they moved in together. In April they married.

*La Esmeralda, Mexico*

It was the street sweeper, with his scraped, spray-painted orange trash barrel behind him on its three-wheeled cart, a crude ocotillo staff sticking up from the barrel. He was knocking at a door. The painted adobe houses along the block were well-kept for the most part. Some had white lintels above their doors and thin wooden spouts extending from their parapets. Wooden shutters were closed on unglassed windows.

The door before which the sweeper stood was bright blue. It was the only blue door on the block. After a while, it was opened from the inside by a man who stood thickly in the doorway.

"Si?"

The sweeper took off his cap and glanced with rheumy eyes into the face of the police chief.

The chief looked at the man's right ear and then at his eyes and then at his ear again. Coming out of his right ear, like a blossom emerging from a cactus flower, was another, smaller ear. That's a weird thing to live with, the chief thought.

The gnarly fingers of the sweeper's hands were holding his cap at the level of his belly. His flannel sleeves swallowed the better part of his hands.

"Hay algo," he said and stopped, as though hoping the police chief might want to finish this sentence himself.

"Si?" The police chief made an effort not to stare at the double ear.

A thin black dog with white paws appeared behind the sweeper. It lifted a leg and urinated against the front wheel of the sweeper's cart, while he stood before the police chief gathering his words.

"Hay una cabeza o algo," he spoke softly to the chief. "En la plaza."

The dog trotted away.

The chief had been looking past the man into the street, its cobblestone replaced last month by concrete; he'd been listening to the roosters crowing in the mud yard on the street's far side and wondering about the man's deformity, but now he searched for the man's eyes. The sweeper lowered them and studied the concrete porch step. Behind him, in the street, a beleaguered mariachi wearing headphones weaved around the trash barrel cart, jousting briefly with the broom staff.

"O algo?" the police chief asked.

The sweeper apparently didn't have anything to add. He didn't meet the chief's eyes again.

The chief left him at the door and went into the bedroom to make a phone call. He picked up his holstered .40 caliber from the chair and strode into the interior garden, buckling the holster around his waist. Canaries and rose finches were chirping in cages hung from pikes in the wall. In the garden, the fountain sparkled, and the tile floor was freshly washed. The chief's wife was talking with the maid at the door of the kitchen, but when she saw his face, she cut off the conversation and came over to where he stood. He was running his hand through his hair, massaging thick tufts at the back of his neck. She looked up at him, waiting.

When the police chief returned to the open front door, the sweeper and his cart were gone. A woman carrying a basket on her back hurried along the sidewalk on the far side of the street, away from the plaza. The chief looked at this watch. It was 6:35, Tuesday morning.

## Ojinaga to Presidio to Langtry

There were no paved Mexican roads across the Chihuahua Desert connecting Ojinaga and Sierra Mojada, so they had to return to Texas to catch the U.S. highway running east above the border. Back in Presidio, Texas, Dale pulled into a Fina station just after noon. In the Win Dixie parking lot across the street, two cop cars were parked alongside each other, front to back, the drivers jawing through their open windows.

As Hoa opened her door, she caught a whiff of herself. It was the second day of wearing her coral blouse and time, she thought, to change it. She asked Dale to lift the trunk and she opened her duffel bag, rummaging around for a crinkly purple polo shirt she bought on a whim at the hotel gift shop in El Paso, thinking Dale would like it.

She walked into the mart and spied the sign for the ladies room around the corner from the drink station. Inside the bathroom, she stood at the grimy sink and looked at herself in the spattered mirror. She didn't want to set down the new shirt on the sink or on the floor so she stuffed it and her purse between her knees, untied the bottom knot, and lifted her blouse over her head quickly, glancing at the door to make sure she had locked it.

Putting the blouse over her purse, still between her knees, she pulled on the purple sleeveless polo, which felt tighter now than when she tried it on in El Paso. She considered herself in the mirror, the worn blouse and purse still gripped between her knees. She looked uncomfortable, she thought. Someone startled her by knocking on the door.

"Just a second," she said.

She quickly checked herself again in the mirror, adjusting her hair but sensing something was askew. The polo wasn't right, it was too thin, too tight. Or maybe she wasn't wearing the right bra. Her breasts looked mashed in the front and rounded at the sides like sponge cakes.

Whoever it was knocked on the door again lower down.

"Just a second," she repeated. She glanced anxiously at herself once more, and plucking up her coral blouse and purse, she turned and opened the door. It was a Mexican woman with her little girl and they all nodded as Hoa stepped out.

"Hola," Hoa said in a friendly voice to the girl, suddenly missing Declan acutely. Seeing him as a boy with his hand in her hand. She felt a stitch in her belly. She was heading toward the glass door when she noticed a stack of little Playmate coolers by the cash register. Adjusting her purse on her shoulder, she picked the blue one on top and set it on the counter by the register.

"Wait a second, un momento," she said to the clerk, embarrassed to hear herself for the second time in a minute using bad Spanish to speak to Americans in Texas. She shouldn't presume anything, she scolded herself, and walked over to the refrigerated section; she slid open the door to grab a couple bottles of water, gratefully accepting the cool air on her face.

An adolescent boy came up behind her while she paid for the cooler and drinks at the counter. She was half-conscious of an exchange of some kind going on between the clerk, probably a high-school student, and the boy behind her. She dropped the change into her purse beside her book, set the bottles in the cooler, and headed for the tinted glass door which opened into a piercing brightness. Pausing there a moment, she overheard the clerk squawk to the teenager, "¿Viste las tetas?"

Dale was putting the nozzle back into the pump, turning his face away from the sweet tang of atomized gas around him. He glanced up to see Hoa marching out of the mart toward him, carrying the little plastic cooler. She yanked open the car door, looking angry, and put two bottles of water into the cup holders between their seats.

Dale slid behind the wheel and started the rental car, pulling out of the Fina, heading the way they'd come. Two Harley Davidsons drew up behind him with their low potato-potato rumble, and Hoa started to say something, but Dale interrupted.

"Just one quick stop." Two blocks up the street, he pulled in at Cheapo Dos Liquors. He left the car turned on with the air conditioning running and, a few minutes later, came out of the store smirking behind his sunglasses, opening the back door on the driver's side.

"What'd you get," Hoa asked with disinterest. He hadn't noticed the new shirt.

He pulled out of the bag an amber fifth of Tres Generaciones tequila, held it out for her to appreciate, and slid his knee onto the back seat to open the cooler on the floor. "Not so cheapo. But we can consecrate your new cooler."

"You want me to drive?" she asked as he got in behind the wheel.

"Sometime. I'm good."

The road was truckless and clear. Hoa took off her seatbelt and leaned forward while the seatbelt alarm chimed. She pulled her new polo over her head. She unballed the coral blouse in her lap, wriggled her arms through the sleeves, then sat back and started tying the front knot.

"I thought—" Dale started.

"I didn't like," she said, reaching for her seatbelt again, tossing the purple shirt into the back seat.

When something was bothering her, Dale noticed that Hoa's lips tightened and her mouth parted just enough so that her teeth showed. It was slightly vampiric.

"I liked," he said.

* * *

The desiccated country rolled out before them. Against background ochers, discrete umber telephone poles snapped by. Screens of creosote bushes sprawled into the desert. Occasional sunstricken buildings beamed off-white and the sky, which was almost colorless at the horizon, blued intensively toward its zenith. They passed a restaurant with a gleaming tin roof, two eighteen-wheelers, and several cattle trucks hulked beside each other in a dirt parking lot. There were long stretches of emptiness, and then a few shacks set back from the highway or what might have been an abandoned gas station.

From the corner of her eye, Hoa watched Dale loosen his grip on the steering wheel. His right hand slid down to five o'clock and, as though feeling the need for balance, he brought his left hand up from his lap and touched three fingers to seven o'clock. Hoa adjusted the air-conditioning vent so it struck her in the forehead. Sitting with her legs crossed in a semi-lotus position, she did her scale pose, pressing her palms to the seat and lifting herself. She held it for half a minute, rocking slightly like a temple bell.

In the early afternoon, modest hills gave way to sloped mesas. There was a sharp curve in the highway. Volcanic massifs drew up in the distance on one side of the car, then the other, and segued to a long run of serrated mountains. No plant Hoa could see grew more than head-high. Traffic raced along lightly in either direction, and Hoa caught Dale checking his speed repeatedly because there was so little to measure it against. As the afternoon wore on, the highway itself seemed to be browning at the center even while it went chalky along the sides.

When they drove through small Texas towns, the speed limit changed and so did the vegetation. There were small cacti and yuccas, a few neon-pink wildflowers, sometimes mesquite trees or oaks around municipal buildings and banks. On either side of Sanderson and Dryden, the north slopes of hills were furred with dry grasses. Once, they passed a faded green motel with heavy plastic curtains where the doors should have been. From the number of cars and pickups parked at the rooms, nose-in like nursing puppies, it looked to Dale like it was doing a brisk business.

The music was on again, and they were talking about whether it was safe to buy a house in Mexico, whether it would be worth doing even though they both knew they couldn't afford one. Hoa had finished her book on Mexico, and she decided to read to Dale for a while from a memoir she had started. It was written by a woman who was a poet, who had a very difficult time bringing up her adolescent boy, an incredible ordeal, worse than what Hoa and Dale had been through with Declan. The writer's boy had been in a gang, had stolen his mother's car when he felt like it, was out all night and slept all day. He only spoke to his mother to curse her. The father was nowhere. But the boy was full of painful tendernesses too. When he came home one night with a runaway friend his own age and insisted his mother let the boy live with them, she acquiesced and raised both of them for two years. She also kept adopting animals—cats and dogs—although she could scarcely afford to feed them. In fact, that was what the poet had learned. To give in, to let it come, to roll with the punches. Precisely what Hoa and Dale knew they hadn't learned in time. Their own son's adolescence had been one continuous, spasmodic argument.

Hoa looked up from her book. Through the spit-size unincorporated town of Langtry, Texas, they were following a black Ford Bronco with rubber bull testicles swinging from its trailer hitch. Remembering Dale had mentioned Langtry earlier, Hoa tried to restrain herself from saying anything about Judge Roy Bean other than to ask if Bean really had said that the law distinguished between a Chinaman and a man.

All the arroyos they crossed were dry, spotted with creosote bushes. It was hard to imagine how the arroyos might look—especially the wide ones—with muddy rainwater slashing through them. At Comstock, they filled up the tank again and crossed the Peco River, which was flowing and ribboned on either side with brushy greenery. Passing through Del Rio, Hoa saw a sign to Ciudad Acuña and asked if that meant Spider City.

Dale wasn't sure what it meant—something to do with coins, he thought, but the word for spider was *araña*.

"You remember that hotel—wasn't it in southwest Virginia?—so infested with spiders?" Hoa asked.

"Fuck, I'll never forget. They didn't want to give us our money back—"

"Even though we didn't even get our luggage into the room," Hoa finished his sentence.

"Hey, is that a buzzard or a hawk?" Dale asked.

It only took her a few seconds. "It's what people call a desert buzzard, but it's really a hawk."

"Got any more water?" Dale asked.

She was missing hearing from her boy.

"I drank it," she said. "I'm ready to call it a day."

## La Esmeralda

The sheriff parked in the street at the edge of the plaza where already a crowd of some fifteen stood mutely, facing the center island with its *Bienvenido a La Esmeralda* sign. He slammed his car door to add authority to his arrival and approached the island. A young boy at the back of the crowd turned and looked up at him and then others turned and stepped sideways to open a corridor through themselves to the island on which had been placed, under the welcome sign and at the edge of the high curb, something unidentifiable, round, and appalling with hair. With, the sheriff realized, a face. That's what it was, a face.

"Dios mío, cuánto cabrón," he said under his breath.

He had entered the crowd and then he must have stopped moving forward. He felt the people around him breathing on his neck.

"Váyanse a casa," he ordered. "Váyanse de inmediato."

Then he had a second thought. "Quíen es?" he asked. But the people had begun to scatter and he heard them chattering, a babble of voices, and he wasn't processing the words.

His deputy's pickup pulled up on the other side of the island. The deputy got out, taking in the scene. Early morning. Men and women and children dispersing from the center of the plaza. The clanking of the metallic conveyor dealing tortillas over burners in the open tortilleria behind him. The scent of baking corn flour. His boss standing alone and unmoving there, like a pilgrim before a relic.

## Crossing the Border Again, Piedras Negras

By the time they got to Eagle Pass, it was almost nine p.m. They were both completely worn out from sitting.

"Rendido," Dale said.

Hoa didn't look at him. It was darkening quickly. The lights of cars in the opposite lane were stabbing her eyes.

"We're rendido," Dale repeated.

Hoa didn't say anything. She sat low in her seat.

She thought they should get a hotel on the U.S. side, but Dale argued the hotel would be cheaper in Mexico, only a few minutes away, and it would be a victory to arrive there. So they crossed into Mexico again at Puente II. The same routine, showing their passports and buying another tourist card and vehicle permit. Trucks were lined up on the bridge going north, but the way south was open. The road took them southeast along the railroad tracks and past a switching station. More trucks were lining up to go north as they merged into an insubstantial traffic pouring into the burning neon night of Piedras Negras. In less than ten minutes, they found a Quality Inn that had a little outdoor pool and a restaurant.

"Fine," Hoa said, unbuckling her seatbelt, "if the restaurant's still open." Her stomach had been growling for the last two hours.

Inside the motel lobby, there was a curved reception counter facing the open doors to a restaurant. There were two restrooms and a luggage room against the far wall and a counter display of silver and turquoise jewelry. The restaurant was still open.

In the men's room, Dale aimed his stream of urine at some toilet paper stuck to the side of the bowl while Hoa stepped into the restaurant and stood at the hostess station listening to American pop music playing from hidden loudspeakers. She didn't recognize the band. It seemed even worse than pop music in the U.S., and she wondered if somehow music that was too pathetic to play on American stations was exported abroad—the way pesticides outlawed in the U.S. were still shipped to third-world countries. On her left, the bar counter stretched away, and through the open service hatch she saw a woman clearly not the bartender, a middle-aged woman in a long white jacket. Pulling bottles from under the bar, she was holding them up and shining a mini-flashlight into them.

The hostess appeared, a young Mexican woman with a plastic red hibiscus pinned to her high chignon.

"Just one?"

"No," Hoa said. "There's two of us." She nodded her head toward the bar. "What's that woman doing?"

"This way," the hostess said. Maybe she hadn't heard the question. Hoa followed her to a booth against the wall as far as possible from the bar.

"What's the woman behind the bar doing?" Hoa asked again, sliding into the booth.

"Ah, la inspectora. Checking for—moscas de la fruta," the hostess whispered, tight-lipped. Then, "Your waiter will be right over." Quick smile, small teeth.

Over dinner, Hoa was too tired and depressed to talk, so she ate and she went ahead and asked Dale about the execution of

Ambrose Bierce in Icamole to get him started. She was ready for any distraction at this point, even Ambrose Bierce.

"You've got to wait until we get to Icamole," Dale said.

"Whose rules are those?"

She used another half a tortilla to wipe the last of the sauce from her plate. The chilaquiles had been served with red frijolitos and chicharrón in chile verde. It had sprinkled cheese and three slices of white onion on top. She swallowed the last bite, sinking back in her booth.

"I don't make the rules," Dale said, putting on his Judge Bean voice. "I just follow 'em."

Something between a smile and a flinch showed on Hoa's lips. She called the waiter over to ask for another Modelo Negro.

"Me too," Dale agreed. "Dos cervezas por favor."

Just before the beer arrived, Dale wiped his eye with a finger tainted by his camarones a la diabla. End of evening. In bed, he lay awake, exhausted, listening to Hoa softly snore, with what felt like a campfire roaring under his right eyelid. He was thinking of Sunday night in Marfa when they were making love, when she broke down and couldn't stop crying. And then he was thinking of a night before then. At home, lying on her side facing him, she had taken his hand and placed it awkwardly on her left breast and said something into his shoulder.

"What?" he had asked

"Do you still mean it, Dale?"

It took him a couple seconds before he answered. "Yes."

## On the Road to Icamole

In the morning, after coffee and huevos rancheros, Hoa went outside
to the car for the Playmate cooler. She carried it past their room to the
ice machine and scooped ice over the fancy bottle of tequila. Right
then, she remembered a part of her dream. Dale was rolling on top of
her and where his nose swiped her face, her skin sparked. He smelled
like autumn. Her hands cupped the angular blades of his back, which
were huge, almost like wings. She and Dale were face to face, breathing the same air. But his mouth opened strangely from the sides of
his head like a dragonfly's. Then his weight lifted, he was gone, she
couldn't find him, and she was cold, looking up at unfamiliar stars.

"Two hundred fifty miles, all good highway, from Nuevo Lar-
edo to Icamole," Dale announced as she slid into the car. He was
reading his maps with his sunglasses on and, she thought, a determined airline-pilot look on his face.

"Want me to drive?"

"Sometime. Not now."

Outside the hotel, they cruised past a crowd of a dozen or so
people waiting for the bus, and then it was another seven hours in
the car with a few breaks for gas and restrooms. Dale drove it all.
Eighteen-wheelers and buses roared toward them in the opposite

lane like testy prehistoric beasts. The hills gave way to benches, arroyos, level stretches of desert clotted with brush and rock and scraggly trees. Crumpled Kraft-paper mountains squatted behind all the flatness. Toward Monclova, the vegetation lushed into various shades of green and yellow. There were trees along the road—oaks, even palms. A fat, burned rump roast of a mountain brooded over the city of Monclova, clouds garnishing its crest.

Through downtown Monclova, they were bumper to bumper. Dale pulled over onto the shoulder at a big construction site where, below a gantry crane, half a dozen blue and aquamarine portable toilets were lined up. They returned to the car and drove on, beyond a corner where people were protesting something, chanting, shouting through a megaphone, banging pots and frying pans, and blowing vuvuzelas with anarchic zeal. At the city limits in a parking lot, a band played in the back of a pickup truck for a crowd of forty or fifty people. Three blocks later, Hoa spotted a busy food stand advertising tacos, enchiladas, and queso fresco. It was only after they ordered that they noticed—hidden behind the crowd of customers and chained to a tree—a huge dust-covered heap of fur, lying listless in the heat.

"Is that a fucking bear?"

"Tomorrow will be easier," Dale said for the second time in as many minutes. He stood behind her, massaging her shoulders, turning her just enough so that the bear wasn't in her field of vision. The traffic was noisy, the air strafed with dust.

"A fucking bear." Hoa's head throbbed. She felt like her brain had been rattling against her skull for the last few hours and Dale's hands felt good. He used to brag, at the beginning of their relationship, that he had his Swedish grandfather's hands, and maybe he did. She felt a ligament in her left shoulder—which she had injured loading the kiln two years before—popping back and forth.

"I can hear that," Dale said. "Does it hurt."

She made a small groan that didn't sound like pain. Then she turned and pulled him against her.

A few feet away, at the edge of the dirt parking lot, a single picnic table was occupied by a middle-aged couple with three children. They were eating tamales. A big plastic bottle of Coke sat at the center of the table. Everyone had a black plastic cup.

Dale picked up their order and they ate, standing in the sun with the food on the trunk of the rental car, since Hoa didn't want to be anywhere near the bear.

Soon Dale was again behind the wheel driving. Only a few minutes had passed when he said, "That one makes an even dozen."

"What?"

"You didn't see that little box with a jar in it and the cross there?"

She looked backward out the window at the side of the highway. She knew what Dale was talking about.

"One of those memento mori?"

"Yeah," Dale said. "*Animitas milagrosas* they're called. I've counted twelve of them today."

"For people who died in car accidents?"

"I guess. Usually there's a cross, and sometimes a little statue of a saint, and the family comes to put flowers there or shoes or cigarettes, all kinds of things."

"For whoever died."

"Yeah. The soul lingers in the place where it was last alive."

Hoa saw mountains looming in the south, bigger ones than any they had passed. An hour or so later, she felt herself leaning forward to make out the words on a highway sign up ahead. V. Garcia 44, Monterrey 84. She glimpsed two young men, ten feet between them, dressed identically in jeans and long-sleeved white shirts. Against the whoosh of passing cars and trucks, each held his white straw cowboy hat to his head with his right hand. She imagined them in a music video.

"We're there," Dale sighed. "Forty-four miles. Icamole's part of Villa Garcia. Just forty-four miles. Check it out on the map."

"Great," she said, underwhelmed. "That's like hearing there's only forty-four more whacks." Nevertheless, she paged through the maps Dale had printed out, and she located Icamole.

Alright, Dale thought. A lot of car time.

From then on, the pavement alternated with long stretches of hardpacked sand and pitted dirt roads. The barren adobe and wattle structures beside the road were roofed with tin or pine branches. There was an occasional painted house, or cinderblock beer mart, and then long stretches of empty space.

It was close to 5:30 when—mutually grumpy, sore, blasted from sitting all day—they finally parked at the dusty Ninja-turtle-green and pumpkin-orange Tienda Campesino in Icamole. The last forty-four miles had cost them two hours with the sun drilling through the car windows and taking its toll despite the air conditioning. Dale felt terrible about how long the drive had been. Wanting Hoa to enjoy the adventure, as he kept calling it, he felt responsible for the trip to turn out well.

Dale slammed the door, shook out one leg, then the other, rolled his neck and then his torso, bending forward low enough to feel the stretch in his lower back. He walked stiffly into the shadowy tienda, mesmerized by the low gleam of cans and bags of snacks. From the dust-caked and barred windows, a dull yellow light spilled over the top row of merchandise. Against the wall, cases of Tecate were piled to the ceiling. Dale felt himself being observed, so he turned to the dueño and offered a *Buen día*. An old man with a gray mustache and a gray baseball cap sat behind the counter with a magazine opened to a full-page photograph of—what was it? It looked like a steer being butchered on a hook, but it was too dark to be sure.

Perdón, but where, Dale asked, could they find La Hacienda de los Muertos?

The man pointed the way with a chile-dusted grasshopper between his fingers. It was up the very street they were on. Derecho, derecho, todo derecho.

When he turned, Dale saw Hoa, with a bottle of Coke in each hand, bending toward a shelf of obscure items in the corner.

"Y los servicios? Dale asked.

The man looked at him uncomprehending.

"Los baños?"

From his shadowy perch, the dueño made a circle motion with the tweaked grasshopper.

Dale walked outside and around the side of the building to a rusty orange door. He opened it, and daylight surged onto a grimy bathroom floor trembling with hundreds and hundreds of daddy longlegs. None of them scurried away. It was as though there were some kind of electric current coming up through the floor and locking them in place. They quivered there en masse, like the entranced members of a horrific cult. Was it part of a mating ritual? Dale shivered reflexively and quickly closed the door. He hurried back inside to find Hoa. She was selecting snacks from one of the racks along the dark wall.

"What's he eating," she asked in an undertone as Dale stepped close.

"Chapulines," he said. The dueño stuck his hand into the plastic bag. "Grasshoppers with chile and lime."

As Hoa was working out the pesos with the dueño, Dale paused outside the doorway. He stuck his head back in and called, "No hay luz adentro?" It was half comment, half question. The store's only light fell in through the open doorway.

"Hay plena luz afuera," the old man responded solemnly.

Dale turned and looked into the street. Yep, he said to himself, there's plenty of light out here.

*La Hacienda de los Muertos*

Outside the tienda, they stood with their open Cokes and an airy bag of picositos that Hoa had immediately torn open. She wondered if they could walk around Icamole for a bit, but Dale said it would be too hot and dusty. There was a little mining museum they could check out after La Hacienda de los Muertos, but they were still going to need to drive back to Monclova to find a place to stay the night.

She asked how he was going to discover anything about Ambrose Bierce if all their stops were scripted, if all they did was step out of the car and get back in. She didn't think she would last through another all-day drive. Dale could see the wave of frustration hit her, and he too was feeling a revulsion for the rental car.

"Look." He tried to be encouraging. "Why don't you drive us out to La Hacienda de los Muertos and we can walk around there."

"How come it's called *de los muertos?*" They were talking as they crossed in front of the broiling hood of the car, switching places.

"So Mexican," Dale said with a big grin inside the car, buckling up. "It's just the site of the old mine. Where everyone lived when Bierce showed up here. *If* Bierce showed up. We'll see anything he might have seen. It's supposed to be beautiful, what I've read."

She drove for the first time on their journey. In the passenger seat, Dale was all the more conscious of the sound of the car on the road, the munch of tires on dirt, although dirt, Dale thought, would be a euphemism. It was packed dust strewn with fragments of rock. In some sections, the road was a puce color and pebbly, and he knew they were going over volcanic strata. The form-marks on many of the outer walls had weathered to look like ripples in sand. Some of the structures were nothing more than heaps of mud. They passed two newer buildings on either side of the street, one painted in earth tones and the other pink with blue trim, but even they seemed mysteriously empty, their doors and windows mortared up. Absolutely no one was on the road.

"They probably lost population to Mina and Garcia until they didn't have enough kids going to school here to support a teacher. Then the rest bailed. But I'm sure there are still people living here, and in caves up there."

In her peripheral vision, she caught Dale pointing with his eyes toward the serrated mountain on her left.

"It's riddled with caves. Natural ones and ones made by miners. That's where a lot of them used to live, anyway." He peered out the side window now at a fenced adobe pen with a donkey inside it.

"Grutas de Garcia are near here. Gorgeous caves. When Bierce came to Icamole, this place was booming. There would have been more than a thousand people running around here. Mining."

The bag of picositos was in Hoa's lap and she used one hand to drive and one to eat the pepper-sprinkled nuts.

"What were they mining, gold?"

"That's my bottle," he said as she picked up his Coke. "No, silver. And later, when the silver played out, zinc."

Behind the wheel, she felt like she had, at last, something to do. A mission. She was sitting up in her seat and more awake than she had been for most of the last two days. Dale noticed the change.

He thought she would get a kick out of the old mining hacienda that some people called La Hacienda del Diablo.

They came at it head on. The road petered out to nothing more than tire tracks across the alkali plain. In front of them, between scrums of creosote bushes, they could see white buildings—some joined and others set off—all silhouetted against the dark mountains. The tallest and most central was obviously the church, and they drove across the hard sand right up to its front door. The closer they got, the clearer it became to them that the buildings were ruins, and only the limestone facade of the church was intact, original. The church's sides had been rebuilt, probably recently. There was a dark wooden cross above the front door and another cross, an iron one, at the peak of the bell tower. But nothing behind the bell tower's facade, Dale could see that. And little was left of the adjacent convent, but for pocked and wind-scarred mud bricks and swabs of adobe plaster. The outlying buildings were in worse shape. Some were just broken walls. To Hoa, they looked like clay shapes molded by a child, with crude gaping doors, notched half walls, and collapsed corners. Like things Declan made as a little boy in her studio.

"This is what I'm talking about," Dale said, his eyes lighting up.

"It's like a cross between Stonehenge and Corbusier," she answered.

"Keep the doors open."

Hoa put the car in park, leaving the keys in the ignition, and they bailed out in front of the church. She thought there might be a breeze in this big open space—this vast plain ringed by mountains glowering with late afternoon—but as she approached the church, she felt none whatsoever.

Without breaking stride, Dale agreed to Hoa's suggestion that they put off seeing the church until last. He followed her around the jumble of outlying walls and hovels. She could be boss for a while, no problem.

Each of them was thinking about the sounds and lives of the people who had once lived here. It was easy for Hoa to imagine them: the streets clamorous with men in hats ignoring or greeting each other, their low voices bouncing from and absorbed by these very adobe walls. A library of irretrievable sound waves. As a potter, she liked that. The thought that infinitesimal traces of human lives were caught in stone and clay. She'd been thrilled when she first heard about archeologists using lasers to try to play back ambient sounds impressed as sonic bands in vases, when potters, thousands of years ago, used cockle shells or pointed sticks to shape the wet, turning clay. Just like wax records. The humming of the pottery wheel, children's laughter, a dog barking. A moment's sound waves injected into clay grooves and locked there as the potter worked. Even if the science wasn't good enough to reproduce the sounds convincingly, she thought it should be possible.

And here, now. She could hear the ghosts of the past. Miners and whores, married couples and their children, who made brief claims against the desert and oblivion. People who, with every muscular contraction, every embrace, every swallow of pulque and water, proclaimed that they themselves were, among all those who had come before them, the only ones privileged to their particular moment. Their now. They were the living. They filled their lungs with dry air, they walked and slept and dreamed. And now, *in her own now,* Hoa thought, not so many years later, those others were snuffed out. And their last readable signs were being subsumed by the desert.

Hoa thought about Declan, but this was a given, a constant, something she simply couldn't help. Like the blue mountains in the distance. She worried about him, and kept the worry to herself. There was nothing Dale could do about it, nothing she could either. She knew Dale was dealing with the same pain, trying to jerrybuild a daily life around the silence of their boy. The last time

Declan had called, Dale had answered the phone and she had repeatedly interrupted Dale's conversation, telling him what to say, what not to say, and finally indicating with hand signals that she needed to talk to Declan herself. But when Dale handed her the phone, Declan had already hung up.

And Dale was, in fact, thinking about their son at the same time. It was likewise something he couldn't help. He wondered what Declan would think of this ghost town, but he didn't want to say anything to Hoa, she had been depressed for so long.

Each protecting the other's vulnerability with their own silence, each carrying the boy privately, and so they bore him together. Their son wasn't simply shared. He was multiplied between them.

\* \* \*

The ground around the hacienda was hard, almost smooth but for mud bricks and parts of bricks that had tumbled out of the walls. They stepped under tenuous, sloped copings and stuck their heads into doorways, into staved openings that had become doorways, and looked at barren, unroofed interiors that precisely resembled the exterior. No birds. No rodents. From a little distance, the corrugated mud walls appeared to be made of cardboard. Inside the walls, the spaces were clean, with little vegetation and no trash. You stepped from the sunlit world under the lintel and entered the sunlit world.

With his phone, Dale was taking photographs of the traces of words painted over an archway. There was the word *ESTAS*, an N, maybe an A, and an I. The letters might have been red once, but they were reduced to a subtle rust-tinged glow, like a car's cigarette lighter just before it goes dark.

Hoa was beside him again, contemplating the illegible letters.

Maybe the last word on the wall, Dale thought, was B A B E L ? Taking a photograph of the ambiguous graffiti, Dale suddenly realized what it said. ESTAS EN BABIA. He had no idea what that meant. You're in Babia? He powered off his phone, watching the white gear spin until the screen went black. Turning his way, Hoa saw he was looking at her, his eyes watery with emotion for just a second.

They looped back to the church where they had parked and Hoa stepped first through the big door, a beautiful piece of carved wood in the weathered marble facade. Standing to one side, urinating into the dust, Dale heard her exclaim, "Ahh."

"Let's see," he called, zipping up. He reached for the folded paper from his back pocket and plucked his pen from the thigh pocket of his cargo pants. He assumed it would be like the rest, a barren enclosure. But the inside of the church had been partly restored: a rectangular room, roofless, its newly whitewashed adobe walls radiant with refracted evening light. Behind the whitewash were pastel traces of old murals. The dirt floor had been swept clean, and someone had laid polished concrete tile in front of an altar. Dale could see a niche decorated with plastic flowers and small statues of saints and sacred-heart candles.

They approached the altar slowly, together, their steps in sync, it occurred to Hoa, like they were supplicants. Above them, instead of a ceiling, there were wisps of cloud and blueing sky. On the floor before the altar, what looked at first to Hoa like glasses of milk turned out to be glasses of white candle wax. The niche of the altar had been painted baby blue, but this had only encouraged graffiti, although some of the words were scraped into illegibility or hidden by judiciously arranged plastic flowers. A hand-written cardboard sign hanging from the wall gave AVISO IMPORTANTE, noting that while the chapel was being rehabilitated, offerings had been removed, but would be returned when the rehabilitation was complete. Dale watched Hoa making her way through the language on the sign.

Then something gleaming on the floor caught Dale's eye. Beside his foot, a concrete tile had been replaced by a marble one. The paler stone seemed to be shining from within, or lit from below, and it was inscribed, *Nuestro hijo se fue con los angeles.* Our child has gone with the angels. The jolt Dale felt was purely personal. Hoa was inspecting the statuary at the altar. Dale called out, maybe a little too loudly for a sacred space, "Let's saddle up, we need a place to sleep tonight."

He headed briskly for the door. When she came out, he said, "Why don't you keep driving, and I'll tell you what happened to Ambrose Bierce here."

"You think we're going to get all the way back to Monclava before it's dark?"

"We'll make it. But we need to get gas."

"I'm completely beat," she said. "And I need a bathroom."

"I'd go here somewhere," Dale said.

"It's not that kind."

"I'd still go here. Do you have any tissue paper?"

She took her purse from the car and walked behind one of the ruins they had first explored, as though someone else might be watching.

Dale stood in the shadow of the church wall thinking about the little unspoken twenty-year contention they had about toilet paper in their bathroom. Hoa would always put the roll on the holder in the *under* position, and Dale would sit down, take off the roll and put it back in the *over* position. Generally, it would stay like that for a few days, a week or two, and then he would find it reversed again with the toilet paper hanging down against the wall. Neither of them had ever mentioned it.

Dale met Hoa walking toward the car.

"Tomorrow's the shortest day, in terms of mileage. If we get back to Monclava tonight, it'll be a lot easier on us mañana. Not to mention, we don't really have any options. Not unless we want to spend the night here."

Hoa looked around. It was evening. The distance was sealed with mountains, the first stars flickering into view. Some strange unexpected sadness penetrated her and pressed against her heart.

* * *

The evening before they started on this trip, Hoa had pulled her Subaru into the garage, closed the door behind her, and studied the long scrape along the right wheel well. A month earlier, backing out, she had run into the side of the garage. If they reported it to the insurance company and took the deductible, their rates would go up. She wrestled a forty-pound bag of potting soil onto the porch, opened the door, turned on the lights in the kitchen, and dropped her purse on the chair at the breakfast nook.

Salad and pasta and pesto sounded all right. She took a look in the refrigerator to see if there were any pine nuts. A minute later, she was still bent over, staring into the refrigerator. What had she been looking for? What was she afflicted with?

Arranging salad fixings on the counter, Hoa glanced out the glass door. Dale's pickup was pulling into the driveway. It was just after six, the driveway in shadow. Generally, Dale tried to take care of all his schoolwork at school. He wanted home to be his "hallowed cove." So he stayed at the university late, grading papers and preparing classes in his one-window office. At home, he would work on his Bierce book at a desk in the basement.

Hoa went to the door and opened it for him. She was wearing the turquoise necklace that Dale had bought her at Christmas, when their lives were pure agony and their son was still in the hospital. Dale was lifting two paper grocery bags and a big green plastic bag from the bed of the pickup. He looked to Hoa like he was dressed for a safari. Cargo pants and a black T-shirt and that thin beige travel vest he'd ordered from a men's catalog.

"Got a roast chicken," he said. "I stopped at Fresh Market. Plus, I inherited an espresso machine from Mike."

The evening was heavy and damp. It wasn't raining, but the air was saturated with tiny drops of water hovering as a mist and gently floating to the ground.

"Why'd he give you his espresso machine?" she asked, taking the plastic bag out of his hand.

He moved past her and put the groceries on the kitchen counter. "Got a new one, I guess. How was your day, you had a firing—no. You've got a firing coming up, right?"

"Yeah, I did the tumble load today. I got to place all the wad balls."

"Want a glass of wine?"

"There's white in the fridge," she said. She put the plastic bag down on the kitchen floor and went to the cabinet to get the only two wine glasses that hadn't broken from a set of six.

"It's like," she started, getting back to Dale's question, putting the groceries away while he uncorked the wine. The familiar choreography of their daily lives. "I don't know. Wherever you wad the piece, you know it's going to leave a mark."

Hoa put the milk and yogurt into the refrigerator. "You spend a lot of time visualizing where you want your wad marks since they're part of what you get in the end."

"Right. What's this pesto out for?" Dale asked.

"Ray wants to build a little anagama now, too. Which would be great."

Dale was pouring the wine and holding one glass out to her.

"You know," he said, "I found the name of the guy who put up that memorial stone in the Sierra Mojada cemetery for Ambrose Bierce. Turns out, he's still around, and he moved back to the States."

Hoa said, "Dale?"

"What?"

"Did you or did you not ask about my day?"

He slid into the chair at the breakfast nook across from her. She could see him trying to backtrack the conversation. He took a long sip from his glass.

"I'm sorry," he said. "I was excited about hunting this guy down."

He poured them both a little more and she clinked his glass.

"Tell me about the little anagama," he said.

"Forget it."

"No, really." He was looking at her earnestly.

She wished she hadn't said anything. Suddenly she didn't want to be talking about kilns or oxidation or glaze and slip. She set her glass on the table, stood up and leaned forward. He stroked the tendon along the left side of her throat with his thumb.

"Kiss," she said.

He stood up awkwardly, feeling it in his lower back, and they both moved around the edge of the table. Dale put his arms all the way around her and squeezed her to him.

"Whoa," Dale said as she started biting his neck, "what's that?!"

"Lamprey kiss," she said, pulling him closer.

One of her fabulous squeaky laughs erupted into his shirt as she rubbed her nose against his chest.

*Desert Music*

He parks near the playing field at the edge of town. Shuts the door
and lights a cigarette, leaning into his truck, his lower back against
the side panel. The back of his head and his hat mirrored behind
him in the tinted window. He can hear the calls, the shouts of
young men floating above the tree-lined scarp. He listens intently,
as though for a special sound or as though he were drawing out a
note of particular merit to him.

As soon as he flicks the butt to the ground, he goes around to
the side of the truck and reaches over the rail into the bed. He
comes down the dirt path to the soccer field with a new soccer
ball in the crook of his elbow, whistling. There's a bulge in the
waistband of his jeans. The playing field is dusty, dust suspended
in the air against the scarp and kept from drifting over it by bleary
oaks. The trees line the rim road like sentinels from a bygone
age. The scene below develops a sepia tone. The man in his long-
sleeves, in his white Bailey hat with its cattleman crown, seems
like a visitor from some other world descending, but at ease there.
He is dressed in jeans and a long-sleeved print shirt. Some of the
players are also wearing long sleeves and baggy jeans, and others
are in shorts or in T-shirts. Only the man with the new soccer ball

has on boots. They are black with white-rooster stitching. When he approaches the playing field—its borders vaguely suggested by four head-sized rocks placed in the corners—he is little interested in the game. Not in the primary game. But beyond the far goal posts—those two vertical palo verde limbs supporting a horizontal third—there is another, less organized game played by the children of the men or their younger brothers or, in one case, a teenage boy mangled by some ill fate limping after the rest.

The man drops his soccer ball into the dirt, kicking it forward with his left foot as he strolls the edge of the playing field. He passes the far goal post and keeps on toward the scrappy kids playing their makeshift game. When two of the boys notice him approaching and pause, straightening up to face in his direction, he boots the new soccer ball to one of them. His long bending shot bounces just once before the midfielder knees the ball into submission. A good sign, the man thinks. He waves as if he knows the boy, and then he turns aside to the taco trailer, El Atoron. It has been set up behind the playing field for as long as anyone can remember. That's where a half dozen of the older, more delinquent boys—los vagos and gandúles—stand around smoking and drinking beer. A place to recruit halcónes. The man buys an orange soda, taking his time, thumbing through a wad of cash as though he cannot find a bill small enough.

*five*

## Out of Delicacy

Reached her
fork toward his plate
to claim a piece
of his poblano
and saw herself in
the mirroring window
behind him. Un-
recognizable. And
she drew back
her fork and sank
low in her seat
as if being pulled by
some personal
nucleus of gravity
away from him.
She thought
that whoever forcefully
smiled out from old,
even recent, photographs
wasn't her but
a dead woman, a woman
who didn't exist
anymore, a woman, a girl
who maybe never
had existed, had never
been known by
anyone, herself
least of all.

## Death of Bierce in Icamole

"So here's how Bierce dies in Icamole," Dale was saying.

They had just hit paved road again and Hoa was driving. It was getting dark now.

"I stay straight, right?" If he distracted her from getting back to Monclova, she was going to leave Dale in Mexico and hitchhike to the border.

"Derecho, derecho, todo derecho," Dale said, mimicking the hand gesture of the man with the grasshopper in the tienda. "Remember? There's nothing but flat desert and straight road."

"Alright, alright," she said. Her blue bungee was around her wrist again. Her hair was down over her shoulders.

"So there's a reporter for the *San Francisco Bulletin*, a guy named George Weeks."

"This is back then?"

"Yeah. 1914, when Bierce disappears. Remember, December 1913 was his last posted mail. When we get to Sierra Mojada, I've got a story about a letter that wasn't posted, but that's tomorrow."

"Look," she said surprised. "That bus is moving over so I can pass."

"It happened with me yesterday too. And some of the big trucks'll do the same."

"That's civil," she said, nodding to herself, appreciative.

"You want to hear this story?"

"Right, tell away."

"So there's this reporter for the *San Francisco Bulletin*, George Weeks. He comes down to Mexico to cover the advance of Pancho Villa's army. Villa's getting lots of press in the U.S., and there's a battle in Torreón, west of here. In the desert."

"It's all desert."

"Chihuahua Desert's big."

Dale took a breath. He took off his sunglasses and looked out the window at the darkness falling into the mountains to the east. The formation closest to them—would you call it a mountain or a mesa, he wondered—stood up from the desert like a huge molar.

"So," he went on. "After the fight in Torreón, this guy Weeks stays around and picks up some work with an English-language newspaper called *The Mexican Review*. One day he's shooting the breeze with the manager, a Mexican named Melero, and he asks if Melero ever happened to come across an American by the name of Ambrose Bierce.

"'Bierce?!' Melero goes apeshit. 'Bierce?!' Of course, he says. They were best buddies. Bierce couldn't speak any Spanish and Melero was the only Mexican in Torreón who could speak fluent English, so they always hung out together. Plus, they were both newspapermen. Melero said Bierce was always asking questions about the revolution. Said he, Melero, really liked the guy.

"'Well,' says Weeks. 'What happened to him, to Bierce? Nobody's heard from him in awhile.'

"Melero says he doesn't know. He'll check with some friends. A month or so passes, and he takes Weeks to meet a former sergeant for Tomas Urbina—one of Pancho Villa's top generals. Urbina is famous for capturing San Luis Potosi from the Federales and now there's an eco-hotel named for him in Patzcuaro."

"And."

"And Urbina's sergeant says Sí, sí, he was with Urbina after Torreón, riding west. They ran into a mule train hauling arms to the Federales in Icamole. Fire fight broke out and most of the Federales escaped into the desert. But Urbina's troops captured one of the Mexican soldiers and a gringo. The gringo didn't speak any Spanish and they assumed he'd been collaborating with the Federales. No questions asked, Villa's soldiers executed him on the spot.

"Then the sergeant describes the gringo. It sounds like Bierce, but to make sure, Weeks pulls out a book-jacket photo of Bierce and the sergeant ID's him right off."

"So we've got a firsthand witness," Hoa said.

"Villa was executing people right and left. In Camargo, he lined up ninety women and a firing squad blew them away for, quote unquote, consorting with the enemy."

"Xái tháng chó đẻ." Hoa's choice Vietnamese curse.

"Anyway, a couple months after Weeks, the *San Francisco Bulletin* sends another reporter to Mexico to verify the story. This guy tracks down the sergeant and the sergeant goes through the same account again, same details. He identifies another photo."

She mulled it over. "So that's how Bierce really died? In Icamole?"

"I'm not saying he didn't die in a detention camp in Marfa, wounded after the Battle of Ojinaga. And you haven't heard about his death in Sierra Mojada yet. But it's very possible he was killed by Pancho Villa's men in Icamole. In the wrong place at the wrong time, when he didn't speak enough Spanish to save himself. An eyewitness report."

"Yeah, but an eyewitness saw him die in the camp at Marfa—that guy who carried him across the river. And someone said he saw him die in the battle at Ojinaga too. Right?"

"There's never any shortage of eyewitnesses in Mexico."

## Monclova to Ocampo

At 8:30 in the morning, it was eighty degrees and there was no moving air. Hoa knew it was just a taste of the heat to come. What she didn't know was that something would happen in a few hours that would alter the whole trip. Alter her marriage.

Back in the passenger seat, she strapped her seatbelt on and almost immediately felt captive and depressed. She took one of her anxiety pills without any water. What had she wanted from this trip, anyway? She'd imagined some intimate time with Dale. She thought the change of routine would do her some good. Take her mind off Declan. But she still thought about him, and now she missed her work and her routine *and* her beauteous, risk-loving son.

Morning was just a pile-up of hours. From the Hotel Cumbre in Monclova to Cuatro Ciénagas, the drive was benign. The scenery failed to rouse her, and the landscape seemed to just recycle its various shades of sienna. At Ocampo, they exited the highway to fill up with gas and get something to eat and drink. They passed under an arched gateway made of sandstone, with letters that spelled *Bienvenido a Ocampo Puerta del Desierto.* On either side of the street, there were long rows of ghostly oak trees, their leaves chalky from dust and their trunks painted white.

"I need a bathroom stop, too," Hoa said. "It's been way too much sitting and way too little …"

"Adventure?" Dale nodded empathetically. "I was looking at the maps this morning. I think we can take a major shortcut back to El Paso once we get to Sierra Mojada."

The hood of the car gleamed and brewed under the primeval sun.

The straight, jacaranda-lined street led them to a church, another structure of pink, tan, and gray rocks locked together in a chunky mortar webbing. They found the gas station next to a green, one-room, octagonal public library.

"You see the bars on the windows of the library?"

Dale was turning off the ignition. "Yeah," he said, even though he only just then glanced through Hoa's window and spotted it. "Maybe it used to be the jail."

Dale searched futilely for the credit-card reader on the fuel pump, and Hoa got out of the car, leaned against the front door, and scrutinized the gas station's open garage. She felt the heat from the car door burn her thigh through her cotton slacks and jumped away like she'd been branded. The mechanic wandered out from the bay, and Dale paid for the gas in pesos.

"You think they have bathrooms inside?"

Dale squinted. They were talking through the shimmer of heat rising from the roof of the car. He was doubtful.

"Let's go ahead and look for a place to have lunch," he suggested. "Then it's less than a hundred miles. Sierra Mojada, end of journey." Saying *end of journey*, he felt better already.

"We can spend the night in Esmeralda, just around the bend from Sierra Mojada. This is going to be the day."

"I'm still going to need a bathroom. That shortcut on the way back gets my vote. Maybe we can spend a day decompressing in El Paso. I don't like being out of phone contact."

*In case Declan calls.* Dale finished her sentence in his head.

When they had driven a few blocks from the gas station, Hoa noticed a little restaurant with a sandwich board advertising lunch specials. Dale wasn't really hungry yet, but he turned the car around and parked a block away in a bank's lot. Ocampo was a medium-sized town with a lot of downtown businesses open and a few people in the streets. There was no sidewalk, so they walked single file, Dale behind Hoa, on the curb until they stepped up onto the concrete patio with its little picnic table. They read the specials on the restaurant sign. Chinese-Mexican food.

"Okay with me," Dale said. It was early for lunch and empty inside but for the waitress, a TV, a large flashing multicolored jukebox, and the ammonia reek of cleaning fluid. Hoa headed for the door marked *Sanitario.*

At the counter, Dale glanced at the menu. Then he turned around toward the open front door. Outside, a gray-bearded man in a gaucho hat and a lime-green guayabera sat down tranquilly at the picnic table, taking the one place shaded by a tree. Cars pulled up at the traffic light, and the old man leaned toward them solicitously, peering through their passenger-side windows.

Hoa came out of the bathroom. She glanced at the menu and ordered tortilla soup and shrimp fritters. Dale stuck to the Mexican side of the menu. Carne asada tacos with pickled red onion, roasted chili, and a tomato-cilantro salsa. Black beans cooked with bacon and beer. When he'd finished ordering, he saw that Hoa had stepped outside. She was sitting at the picnic table on the other side from the local man. Dale could see wiry gray hair under his hat. His back was turned to Hoa as though he were too shy to acknowledge strangers.

Dale came over to the table holding two plastic cups of warm Coke and a bag of peanuts. He sat on the bench next to the man and offered a hello toward the back of him. Hoa picked up her drink and made a toasting gesture.

"To the dust in our throats," she said to Dale, "and to a dead Chinaman." Straightfaced.

He opened the bag of peanuts on the table and pushed some over toward Hoa. They had each eaten a few when the local man turned around. As if he had been wondering for hours, he asked if they were English.

"American," Dale answered.

The man said something that Dale didn't understand, then he repeated it. Something about the economy.

"What," Dale asked? In Spanish he said, "I can't understand you."

The local man repeated it more loudly. Just when did Dale think the economy would recover.

"I don't know," Dale answered, surprised. "A year or so? What do you think?" He offered the man some peanuts and the man held out his hand and took them. A few dropped onto the pavement under the bench.

The gray-haired man declared that the economy would never recover.

"So what's next then?" Dale asked.

"Anarchy," he said. Then he said something else difficult for Dale to understand, and he stood up. He peered down at Dale and he asked if he was Jewish.

Dale was aware of Hoa suddenly looking up from her little pile of peanut shells.

"Am I Jewish?"

"Do you have Jewish blood?"

"I don't think so."

"You're not a Jew?"

Dale wanted to catch Hoa's eyes, to give her a look, to raise his brows, but the man had him locked in.

"Why do you want to know if I'm a Jew?"

The man had moved to the head of the picnic table, with his

back toward the restaurant entrance. He was pulling at his beard. Below his green shirt, he was wearing canvas pants and tire-tread sandals. He said something that was hard for Dale to comprehend, maybe on account of his accent, but Dale could tell it had to do with Jews and the economic collapse.

"I don't know," Dale said in Spanish. "Is that what you think?"

Dale was tense now, watching carefully to see how the man would react. The Mexican was looming in front of them at the head of the picnic table, his eyes animated, with dark brown irises, the whites yellowing around the edges. His body was rocking.

For the first time, Hoa spoke up. Not to the Mexican, but to Dale. She said, "Why do you engage him?"

The old man leered her way, asking her if Dale was a Jew. Dale didn't know whether Hoa understood the Spanish, but she answered in English. "Yes, we're Jewish. We don't want to talk to you."

The man exploded, his arms windmilling. He was shouting incomprehensibly, but what he said wasn't the kind of thing that needed translation.

Hoa repeated stubbornly, clearly in English, "We don't want to talk to you, go away."

But the man had more to say. Then, like some gnome in a folktale, he whirled and stomped into the restaurant to vent his outrage at the waitress. From where he was sitting outside, Dale understood that the man was saying one of them had denied being a Jew and the other admitted it.

Hoa reined in Dale's attention. "Why do you engage people like that? You demean yourself. It's patronizing."

Dale felt like he'd run into a tree. Stunned by what had just happened with the man, he was shocked all over again by Hoa's reaction. Backpedaling while he tried to sort it out in his head, he said, "Half the time I didn't know what he was saying."

"You could tell what he was saying. I could tell."

Dale's defenses kicked in. "I listen to people. You learn things that way."

"There was nothing to learn," she said. "You think you were going to learn something from him about the economy?"

Dale angled for a way out. "Look," he said, "I've been in bars and met guys who passed me KKK coins and I let them talk, I wanted to hear how they thought."

"It's not interesting," she insisted. "Racism isn't interesting. Stupidity isn't interesting."

A dark sparrow landed on the concrete, crouched, one-eyed them, and then turned its head sideways and studied the fallen peanuts under the table.

"You find out about how other people think," Dale argued, but he knew she could hear the defeat in his voice. He could hear it.

"You could tell right away. You're just pandering to your need for people to like you."

That brought Dale up short.

"That's what you did with Declan. You wanted to be his friend, and you didn't know how to be his father. You were afraid to be firm, you left it to me so you could ... So he'd *like* you."

Her eyes had welled, and now tears came over the lower eyelids. She grabbed a napkin and turned away on the bench, moving one leg to the other side. Facing the street, she wiped at the corners of her eyes.

The waitress came out and set the shrimp chips in front of her. The sparrow flew off. The chips were blue and yellow and looked like Styrofoam. Silently, the waitress turned around and returned a minute later with Dale's tacos and beans. The man in the guayabera was sitting at the counter inside looking at the TV. Then he came back out, agitated, and he sat at the far end of the picnic table with his back to them both, as though he were sulking. Suddenly,

Dale realized that the Mexican was manning the trundle cart ten feet away on the street. He hadn't noticed it before. There were stacks of newspapers with rocks on them.

Hoa stayed sitting sideways on the bench, picking at her food mutely. When the traffic light changed, a clean, white Chevy pickup stopped at the curb, and the old man jumped up, plucked a newspaper from under the rock, and shoved it through the open passenger-side window to the driver. They were speaking to each other, and Dale wondered how the old guy knew the man in the truck wanted a paper. He watched Hoa taste her soup. They didn't speak to each other. A bespectacled young man in a white pharmacy jacket walked over and bought a paper from the gray-bearded hawker. They exchanged a few words, and the guy in the white jacket ran his hand through his slicked hair, glancing nervously at Hoa and Dale before he re-crossed the street.

Hoa looked into the restaurant where the television was blaring by the counter. Dale considered the miscellaneous storefronts on the far side of the street. A beauty parlor. A pharmacy. A tire bay. A few cars went by in either direction. Four or five pedestrians were walking in the sun.

Now, the old man, Dale, and Hoa sat at the same table staring in three different directions. Like cattle, Hoa thought. About the time she finished her chips and soup, the waitress brought Dale some salted radishes and cucumbers. Dale asked Hoa to go ahead and pay, so she followed the waitress into the restaurant and sat on a stool at the counter inside. She stared at a music video on television while the waitress took forever making change.

Dale ate a few bites of his tacos and beans. The Mexican man said something to him using the word *repugnante,* and Dale stood up, carrying his plate inside to the counter. He put it down. Beside the plate, he left a few coins.

When he came out of the bathroom, he and Hoa walked together out of the restaurant. Dale made an effort to ignore the paper hawker who was pointedly inspecting them. They walked the narrow edge of the dusty street back to their car, single file again, without speaking.

## Toward La Esmeralda

For the next five hours, they let themselves steep in a cenote of silence. In the discomfort and brooding that follows confrontation, they sat next to each other in a dead space with the omnipresent sun melting the windshield. The episode at the lunch table looped through Dale's mind, even as he forced himself to make comments now and then about the scenery, about anything else, in a voice that he tried to adjust so that he didn't sound defensive or hurt. Hoa's accusations, he told himself, were merely the product of long, relentless miles through the desert, the cramped confines of the car, and a wound they both carried. Her lashing out at him in that way was just so much water under the bridge. But every word he spoke sounded stilted or testy, and they sat two feet away from each other like strangers on a bus. And once again, the drive was taking far longer than he anticipated.

The paved road degraded into what they called in rural North Carolina "improved road" and the "improved road" yielded to a swervy runnel of gravel, sand, and potholes that went on chirring and dinging the underchassis for miles. At the side of a dirt road in the sun, they saw a brown dog sitting beside a dead dog that looked at lot like it. The living dog looked directly at Hoa as the car passed. Their eyes locked, each of them thinking what?

Hoa was sick, regretting what she'd said to Dale. But she couldn't say anything more. The bouncing and jolting, the dog and the sun, all made her feel punch-drunk. *Once it goes out of tune,* she thought, *it takes a long time to readjust the quiet to the sound of me.* The trail bent south, and they climbed into mountains slashed by dark plutonic seams and glimmering quartz veins. From the corner of his eye, anxious about her, Dale could see Hoa lean one way and the other as he maneuvered slow twists in the graded dirt road unspooling between calamitous drops and intimidating masses of metamorphic rock.

"What are we averaging, fifteen miles an hour?" Hoa asked matter of factly. Her voice sounded gargled with the car's shuddering. Her first words since lunch. "There's no way trucks with ore from Sierra Mojada could be using this road."

He was quiet a moment, studying her with narrowed eyes behind his sunglasses. Was that more exasperation and weariness in her voice? Was she simply trying to make conversation? She turned to her window.

"I don't know," Dale said. They hadn't glimpsed a pueblo since Ocampo. In fact, they'd seen few human structures at all, but for occasional barbed-wire fences and cattle guards, or smaller dirt roads that led, he supposed, to ranches, although whether that meant wide tracts of fenced desert or little compounds where someone actually lived, he wasn't sure. Sometimes modest adobe houses were visible, limned by dusty mesquite trees, or by stunted, thin-boled oaks.

They descended slowly along that guttered track near a throng of scraggly trees and onto a plain where they joined paved road again. The hues slowly shifted as they crossed what seemed to Dale to be a sparse prehistoric sea floor. On the driver's side into the distance, sets of small brown dunes paralleled the road. On the passenger side, a broad alkaline plain stretched out into mirage and glimmer. Up ahead, a black volcanic cordon oriented them, pulling them slowly forward across the wan vastation. As they drew nearer to the ancient volcano, the road began to curl north around its wide base.

"There's probably another road," Dale said, picking up the conversation that he had dropped several minutes earlier. He felt sunburn on his forearm and stuck his arm under the steering wheel. "Another road for trucks from the mine."

Hoa came out of a trance thinking she couldn't stand to be in the car a minute longer. At first, she didn't know what Dale was talking about. Her throat was scratchy and her eyes itched. She plugged her phone into the console port and scrolled through her music.

"I guess they have a railroad for the ore," Dale went on. "They probably use that."

"Hey, Hoa, you don't want to rub your eyes like that," he added.

She stopped rubbing her eyelids. When she glanced at Dale, she saw that his face had taken on a faint phosphorescence. Somehow, the fine dust on the road was being sucked into the car, and Dale looked a little like a butoh dancer. She lifted her legs and sat cross-legged again, her right knee jammed uncomfortably against the door's armrest.

The landscape around them continued its slow transformations. On the far side of the volcanic upthrust, there were flattened hills of brush, through which sand barely showed. In the distance, there were moonscapes of raw gashed mountains, gnarly buttes of andesite. The road darkened and rose as small cacti and yucca and grasses appeared and disappeared. The tires bounced. Over stones and pits, the car jolted its two bleary passengers.

Another roadrunner. Hoa was amazed by its size. It loped along in front of them for several hundred yards, then swerved behind a clump of sotol and let them pass. Dale overheard her speaking to it, as though she were leaving an old girlfriend. "Bye-bye road-runner."

The next long stretch of road spooled between wide bays of sand rippled by paleo-winds. The road was covered in several inches of powder that, even though the windows were closed and the air conditioning on, continued to find its way into the car. Now Dale could taste it. The hood of the car took on a patina.

He reached into his pocket for his phone, which felt like it was vibrating. Blank screen, it was turned off.

Hoa looked at Dale look at his phone. Thinking of Declan, she turned her face to the side window again. Nothing grew out there. For several miles, a few black strands of wire connected vaguely vertical Palo-Colorado fenceposts spaced every ten feet. The horizon was an uninterrupted panorama of postcard mountains. Hoa readjusted the air vents in the middle of the dashboard so they blew more in the direction of her chest.

They crossed a bench and began to climb a dirt and gravel road. Ahead, the hills took up again, but steeper and more rugged, spewed with artemisia and mesquite. Here and there, they made out the black mouth of a cave or old cinnabar mine. The car zig-zagged at a snail's pace through the switchbacks. Dale's neck and shoulders ached. He was feeling battered, physically and emotionally.

Driving out of the hills, they reached pavement once again. The asphalt was whited with tire-marked dust. There must have been magnesium or mica in the dust because for about twenty minutes, at the angle the sun was hitting the road, it glowed ethereally, as though an archaic hallowed dimension were rising from the place where the road had been.

Hoa asked Dale to stop. While he was putting the car into park, she jumped out, yanked down her pants, and squatted to pee at

127

the edge of road while John Abercrombie's eerie "Show of Hands" carried through the open door into the desert. A strange sound to let out in this place, Dale thought. He got out too and stood by the front door, leaving the car running, rolling his neck, stretching, and looking around. There was a crick in his lower back. Ahead, a pair of crested quail scuttled around a mound of rock.

Invisible on the other side of the car, Hoa hooted.

"What?" Dale checked for her across the car roof. That was the most spirited she had sounded since lunch. But she was still squatting. There were reddish mountains far across the desert on her side. Along the road, rocks and clumps of ocotillo and sotol.

"You okay?" he called over the dusty roof. It had sounded to him like a happy hoot. Maybe she was ready to let the tension go.

"I burned my tush," she explained, standing and buttoning her slacks, then scrambling into the car again. Dale got back in and closed the door. All the air conditioning had been sucked out and it felt like they were sitting upright in a coffin.

"The road's scorching. Wow," Hoa said. "When you get close you can hear the tar hissing."

The buoyancy in her voice lifted Dale out of a dark hole. Maybe the mood was lifting. But he had been mulling over their weird exchange at lunch for hours. He knew there were awful strains inside them both. Each of them harbored a shameful, still unconfessed sense of responsibility for what had happened to Declan, for his accident and his lack of communication. Still, Dale had come to think that Hoa was right about some of what she'd said at lunch. That he engaged with people out of some default politeness that prevented him from distinguishing what mattered from what didn't. That at some point, what he liked to consider his friendliness and generosity to others passed over into a lack of respect for his own time, his own needs. It was the kind of observation she must have noted long ago and lugged around for years, forgiving him, looking beyond it to his better qualities, but nevertheless seeing the evidence mount.

Had he wanted to be a friend more than a father to their son? Neither he nor Hoa had been able to figure out how to handle Declan. When he was charged with shoplifting, Declan, instead of being apologetic, was furious with them both for colluding with the lawyer, even though the lawyer, whom they hired to help, got him off with community service. Yet Declan could be sweet to strangers, to his grandparents. He once spent hours digging out a dead hedge in Dale's father's yard, planting forsythia and box-woods. Declan would give any of his friends the shirt off his back. But in twenty years, Dale couldn't think of a time when Declan had ever apologized for something. Declan held to the way he saw things, with a tenacity that repelled even the possibility of other points of view.

Now that Hoa had said what she said, had dumped the bad onto him, what was he to do? Should he have taken her critique so seriously? Lacerated by all that had gone down with their son, he knew that they had said things to each other in the last six months that weren't true, things they didn't really believe. Still, Dale felt that their dynamic had shifted along a hairline crack, and he wasn't sure how to recuperate himself—not just in her eyes, but in his own—except over some long reconstructive period that was dreadful to contemplate.

*Incident in La Esmeralda*

In the early evening, they entered the township of La Esmeralda, eight miles from Sierra Mojada. The town's name, spelled on the rusty once-reflective road sign was illegible, peppered with bullet holes. They passed a lonely, old hacienda that leaned toward La Esmeralda as though into a wind, its grand adobe walls the same toasted brown as the desert, its many windows and doors boarded up. As Dale drove on, Hoa looked back at it in the hard light. It reminded her of something from *Pedro Paramo.* Closer to the center of La Esmeralda, the hand-poured concrete street had been laid within inches of the walls and doors of the casas and tiendas. There were open lots of sand, nondescript buildings, and adobe houses. Dale drove toward what he figured was the central plaza, guided by the presence of a white tower, twice as tall as any other building, with a prison-green cupola. They both peered up through the windshield at it.

"Not many people out, are there?" Hoa said as Dale negotiated a traffic island dotted with dead shrubs and a sign that said *Bienvenido a La Esmeralda.* On the other side, there was an open tortilleria and the sound of clanking machinery, but no one visible inside.

"Pretty desolate."

"We're almost there?"

"I think Sierra Mojada's only about ten minutes from here."

They passed an empty dirt playground with swings and a red slide protected by shade trees, and came to an intersection with metal-studded speed bumps. A flock of some fifteen or twenty goats drifted diagonally across the street, no herder in sight. Two bleating goats, separated from the main group, came bolting anxiously from behind. Dale kept his foot on the brake and peered in both directions. There were cars and trucks parked along the streets, but not one was moving. Up ahead, a man in a dark, long-sleeved shirt turned the corner toward the tower with the cupola. Dale took his foot from the brake and turned at the same corner. He immediately swung the car to the side of the street, parking it behind a shiny red Dodge Ram with cattle racks in the bed.

"What's up?" Hoa asked, sitting forward in her seat, taking in a crowd of people blocking the street ahead. At the fringes, toward the back, there were women holding the hands of children and small clusters of men talking to each other or hurrying to and from the larger crowd as though carrying messages. Everyone was staring at whatever was going on in the park beneath the tower. It was a clock tower, Hoa noticed, and under the green cupola, the silver hands on the stucco read 5:22.

"I can't tell." Dale turned off the car, opening his door. "Something big."

Hoa came around the front of the car and stood with Dale, both of them wearing sunglasses, watching the crowd milling about. Three men driving a splintery field wagon behind them stopped and got out and hobbled their mules.

The little park was bordered by permanent concrete barricades separated by black wrought-iron benches facing the interior. All Hoa could make out, standing on her toes on the curb and peering through the crowd, were the shapes of trees and lamps in the park.

"Why don't you ask someone?" Hoa said.

Dale took a few steps forward. Several bystanders looked his way as though they heard him coming. Taking off his sunglasses, he approached a short old man with a cane and bowed legs.

"Perdón, señor," he said, his hands in his pockets. "Qué pasa?"

In a high, toothless Spanish, keeping his gaze averted from Dale, the elder replied that they were just now taking the bags away.

"What bags?"

A swarthy man with slicked back hair peered intimidatingly over the older man's shoulder.

Dale stood beside the old man, looking with him toward the park.

"What's in the bags?" Dale asked.

No one answered him. A ribby brown dog with hanging teats limped along the side of the street away from the tumult.

Suddenly the crowd moved as an organism with a swishing and clucking sound, creating a breach in itself at the entrance to the park just below the clock tower. A mule began to bray as though someone were flaying it. Into the clearing, a uniformed man wearing a red paisley bandana over his mouth strode purposively out of the park and stepped down from the curb onto the street. A stout man with thick curly hair and an air of authority, he was searching for someone or something. All eyes were on him. Dale glanced down the street in the direction of the rental car and the wooden field wagon. One of the drivers had also stepped into the street, and now he raised his hand to the sheriff as though he were taking a pledge before the hobbled mules. In the wagon seat, the second driver stood up and took off his hat and placed it over his chest.

The old man next to Dale sucked in his cheeks and blew out wheezily. "Jesu Cristo," he coughed and spat.

Dale turned to follow the old man's eyes toward the park entrance. The sheriff had lowered the bandana from his mouth and was giving instructions to a deputy. Behind the sheriff, two men struggled with a heavy black trash bag. One wrestled with the tied mouth of the bag while the other held the opposite end by its edges. Whatever was in the bag had slumped to the center, and because neither man had a grip on the contents, the bunched and sagging plastic threatened to break. They put the bag down at the curb, one of the men preoccupied by something on his trousers, the other wheeling back toward the park entrance to see how two porters behind him were managing their load. The second pair lifted and swung their own bag forward two feet at a time, letting it drop to the ground between heaves. They did this repeatedly, passing the first men and their bag. The crowd went silent and shifted silently to give them room. With their backs bent, the second two men swung their bag a few feet forward at a time up the calle central to the mule-drawn wagon, which now faced away from the park. Both drivers helped the two men lift the bag into the wood-slatted bed. A dog was barking furiously.

Meanwhile, Hoa came up to where Dale was standing.

"What's going on," she asked in a whisper, inclining toward him.

"Some bags they're hauling out of the park."

"Bags of what?"

The man with the slicked-back hair turned his ear toward them. The old man Dale had engaged earlier propelled himself away on his cane, replaced by a swarm of teenage boys. Three men with grime-stained hands drifted up behind Hoa. There were more than a hundred people clustered around the park entrance now, and they began to chatter again in a rising polyphonous clamor.

Under the direction of the sheriff, a third pair of men emerged from between the concrete barriers, struggling with another slippery garbage bag. The setting sun caught itself on the minaret of the clock tower. The dog that had been barking shrieked three times in decrescendo. Dale felt his phone vibrate in his pocket and checked it, but the face was dark, it was turned off.

"Maybe we should go," Dale said.

* * *

Ten miles further on, they thumped across uneven railroad tracks at an abandoned station. The entire side of a large, concrete barn was painted with a Dreamsickle-orange advertisement. An array of Corona bottles with lime wedges fanned-out like playing cards from a central Corona Extra. After another half mile, the paved road forked and a road sign pointed them toward Sierra Mojada. Still, it was another fifteen unendurably slow minutes before they entered a broad valley ringed by knuckled mitts of stone. The road straightened, and a sprawling town came into view. The sudden display of painted structures—white and turquoise and umber in faded pastels—made Hoa almost giddy.

By then, shadows were digging long black gouges in the mountains around them.

"Can you stand to see the cemetery first?" Dale asked. "And then we get something to eat and then the hotel?"

"Just as long as we get out of this fucking car."

"That's the point." He smiled for the first time in hours.

"So what was going on back there?" Hoa asked. "I know they decapitate people, the drug dealers. And the heads show up somewhere and the bodies show up somewhere else."

"Not really around here," Dale tried to sound authoritative and change the subject. "Bierce writes about that."

"About what?"

"I don't mean the drug stuff. He wrote a book called *Write It Right*. A dictionary of misused terms."

"I don't get the connection."

"Oh," Dale shrugged. "Just something that clicked in my head. Bierce says it's wrong to say the *body* was here and the *head* over there. Because the body's the whole physical person. Including the head. So you say the trunk of the body is over there. And the trunk can include the limbs. Anatomically ..."

"Anatomically?" Hoa repeated.

"Yeah, anatomically the trunk's just the torso."

## Death of Bierce in Sierra Mojada

From the cemetery, Dale drove them back to town with loose stones crunching and yellow dust billowing behind them. People were out on the streets, matrons in embroidered skirts and, incredibly, sweaters. There were younger women in jeans and men driving pickups, their lined brown faces shadowed under gaucho hats. Dale turned off the AC, rolled down the windows, and the heat rushed in like a sigh. Hoa rested her elbow on the open window edge. Lace curtains, fixed with drawing pins, blocked her view into rooms in which she could hear, along every block, televisions blasting.

They followed a pickup past a church to a plaza which Dale circled in order to get a second look at three boys sitting hunched together on the high curb on the center island: two white shirts and a red one. They were casting glances at a deflated soccer ball that lay a few feet away like an expired pet.

Dale parked the car adjacent to the church, behind a Dodge Ram not merely dusty, but sealed in a carapace of baked earth. He retained an adolescent pride in his smooth parallel parking, a talent measured, he once told Hoa, like Japanese brush paintings, in terms of the fewest number of necessary strokes.

Hoa heard him crank the emergency brake as she stepped out, on Sierra Mojada's hand-poured concrete street, into the durable heat of early evening. Halfway to the curb on the other side, she sensed Dale balking as he came around the front of the car. She turned to see what made him pause in the street. Both of them stopped in their tracks to absorb this new view of the town's patron mountain. At the far end of the perfectly straight street, it seemed to have rushed up on Sierra Mojada with the sovereignty of a checkmate. It loomed over the modest spread of houses like a great throne or, indeed, like a queen at whose feet a weary citizenry groveled. The mountain's buff and green peaks were topped by a pompadour of wispy clouds. Visible through pockets in the clouds and extending infinitely, the sky itself was not to be outdone for its sheer expanse.

"Know why it's blue?"

"What do you mean?" Dale said.

"Because blue light ..."

"Oh right," Dale interrupted. "It scatters in the atmosphere more than red light."

"How'd you know that?"

"You told me before."

Hoa took a deep breath, turning from the mountain. Two stout Indian women in traditional skirts and shawls were climbing over the gate into the bed of a clean GMC truck, its cab windows rolled up and tinted. Dale followed Hoa across the street behind the truck to a sidewalk that paralleled an adobe wall. He could hear a child crying.

He stumbled on an uneven crack in the sidewalk. Christ, he thought, I'm beat. Staring at Hoa's back, he lifted his right arm over his head, sniffing his armpit, intrigued by the odor, at once strange and recognized. Passing a swept-dirt courtyard, Dale looked at a playground with a colorful plastic jungle gym, a swing set, red and green slides, and a whirl-around. Something about the plastic colors and the sand made Dale think of an aquarium, a very dry aquarium. There was a turquoise bench too. It was an elementary school, no doubt. The colors were quickly fading in the dimming light and a tinny music—where was it coming from?—filled Dale with a kind of distracted sadness.

"Here," Hoa said, ebullient, nodding across the street. "This is it."

It was a one-door, one-window adobe house with a small block-letter sign by the door reading *Barbacoa*. Hoa's delight that, en route to the cemetery, she had spied such a promising bodegón was obvious in her gait as she crossed the street, her blouse—from the yoke to the waist—sweat-dark along the length of her spine.

One other couple was seated inside, eating at the table closest to the door, where any rumor of a breeze might be picked up. They had clear plastic cups half full of an orange drink. As the woman put her fork down, it tinked against her plate. Hoa wondered if she had been fighting with her husband. Her face was round but pinched at the eyes, and she stared distrustfully at Hoa across the table as though Hoa had entered with no intention but to spread a disease. Her husband was plying his fork in little circles over his empty plate.

Dale came in behind her, nodding at the couple, as Hoa pulled back a chair at a table beneath a small, high, missing-cinderblock window. Neither she nor Dale had taken into account the table's proximity to the mounted speaker on the wall. There was a pause between songs when they entered and as soon as they were settled at the white plastic table, the speaker began blasting corridos into the small room.

A round unsmiling woman in a brown apron—her hair pulled back and knotted in a tight ball—stepped from the back-room kitchen and greeted them. There were no menus. The choices? There were no choices. The barbecue was carne de res. It came with rice, beans, and corn tortillas. They asked for Cokes, and the woman nodded, starting toward the kitchen.

"Perdón, señora," Dale called. The woman took two steps back to the table and leaned toward them with her ear.

"Qué es eso?" he asked. "Detrás de la música. Esa *screek, screek, screek, screek.*"

The woman came a few steps closer. She looked up at the speaker mounted near the small window and listened. For that brief moment, in the soft mix of artificial and evening light, she reminded Dale of a painting. Across the table from him, Hoa was listening too, her eyes following those of the woman toward the opening in the cinderblock wall. There was a strange electronic wail behind the beat of the corrido. Repetitive. At first it sounded like a scratch in the recording, but then it would pause or adjust its tempo.

"Es un sapo de bolsa," the waitress said, her face serious.

"¿Como?"

"Un sapo de bolsa," she iterated in a certain, matter-of-fact tone.

"Gracias," Dale replied.

"A what?" Hoa asked.

"A toad with a sack." Dale stood up to better see through the opening. The couple at the other table was staring at him, and he sat down again.

"I guess there's lots of species of toads in the desert," Hoa was thinking aloud. "This little guy must be just outside the window hole. I wonder if he thinks he's competing with the corridos for his girlfriend."

She was concentrating, cueing in its song, if that's what you'd call it. *Screek screek screek screek.*

"Athletic sucker isn't it?" Dale reached into his pants pocket. "If he's competing with the corrido, he's going to die exhausted and unfucked."

He glanced at the couple at the other table, hoping they hadn't overheard him.

"If I don't eat soon, so will I," Hoa said. "Die exhausted."

Dale was pulling his phone from his cargo pants pocket. He quickly looked up for her eyes, but she had twisted in her chair toward the kitchen to cross her legs.

"I'll try not to let that happen," he said. "Either of those things."

"Let's see the photos of Bierce's grave," she said.

"Cenotaph," he said, lowering his voice, the furrow deepening in his brow. "Bierce's body isn't there."

Hoa leaned her elbows on the table without moving her chair forward. In her awareness, the music shifted to background and what she heard instead was the toad wailing. She wasn't sure she was capable of feeling normal or of carrying on naturally with Dale while some gulf separated them from their child. On Dale's phone on the table, she could make out a good shot of the entrance to the cemetery, the rocky parking area, the knee-high adobe wall, and the sweeping, smooth brown skirt of the mountain.

Dale held his hand out so she could see better and he scrolled to the next image, a close up of the plaque on Bierce's cenotaph.

"Testigos," Hoa was remembering. The script in the photo was too small to read. "Testigos muy confiables ... how does it go?"

Dale zoomed in and read it for her. "Testigos muy confiables suponen. Que aquí yacen los restos. . . Very reliable witnesses believe that here lie the remains of Ambrose Gwinnett Bierce, 1842–1914, famous writer and American journalist, who, suspected of being a spy, was shot and buried in this place."

"Right. But no eyewitnesses?"

The dueña brought out two clear plastic cups filled with ice and orange Fanta, not Coke.

"Oh," said Hoa, adjusting. "I forgot to ask for no ice." She glanced at the dueña and saw that she understood, and then Hoa regretted saying anything.

Dale picked up his cup. "The ice is good here," he said. "To Ambrose."

Hoa picked up her plastic cup and ticked it against his.

Dale took a sip to complete the ceremony, setting the cup on the table, and said, "I'm going to wash my hands."

The dueña was attending to the other table. Talking conspiratorially with the couple.

"Los servicios?" Dale asked to be polite, but he knew they could only be in one direction.

The dueña looked at him blankly.

"El baño?" He was never quite sure which word to use. He could hear the motor of the refrigerator in the kitchen, and he could smell beans and fried meat.

Through the arch, she indicated with her hand. "A la izquierda," she said.

He opened the door and turned on the wall switch just in time to see a mouse run straight up the concrete wall and disappear into a crack at the ceiling. Impressive. It hadn't climbed, it had raced up the wall. Dale stepped toward the toilet. The wall was ordinary concrete, no more rough than what you'd see anywhere. And the mouse had left a little trail of brown urine marking its ascent.

There was just enough room for a toilet, a sink, and a wastebasket. On the wall behind the sink, instead of a mirror, there was a framed print of the Last Supper. Dale lifted the toilet seat with the toe of his boot, but the seat wouldn't stay. He was compelled to keep his left boot up against the stained underside of the seat while he urinated. Still holding the seat back with his toe, he bent to tear off a piece of toilet paper, wiped himself and the rim, then dropped the paper in the bowl. He turned on the faucet and rinsed his hands and face under tepid yellow water. He pumped the lever of a paper dispenser three quick times and it wheezed like a bulldog, but no paper came out. He pulled his shirt up to his face. When he returned to the table, wiping his hands against the thighs of his cargo pants, he saw that the other couple had gone. Hoa was squeezing lens drops into her eyes.

"How do you feel?" she asked, inspecting his mouth for any signs of damage she may have inflicted.

"I'm okay," he said, wanting to turn the conversation away from the incident at lunchtime and the way it had swallowed the rest of the afternoon. "The lowest point today was remembering it's Father's Day this weekend."

She'd forgotten. It was Wednesday evening, and Father's Day would be Sunday. She gave him space to continue.

"I remember last year. The hours going by and he didn't call."

*Entre Chien et Loup*

When they walked out of the bodegón, Hoa paused on the side-walk, checking out the empty street, taking it in.

"It's the hour *entre chien et le loup*," she remembered. "Do the Mexicans have an expression like that?"

"Don't know."

A mockingbird, staying up late, carried on a risible argument with itself in different voices. What was it the Mexicans called them? Dale wondered.

They walked toward the car the way they had come, but this time the street was deserted and quiet. After the intense heat of the afternoon, there had arrived a perceptible slackening of the temperature. It was getting dark quickly, and the nearly full moon floated in a broth of stars.

They were passing the aquarium playground. A boy of about ten was in one of the three swings, sitting, looking their way.

Hoa opened the gate and greeted the boy.

"Buenas noches," she offered.

Dale followed up, although he felt pummeled by the road, tired, and he definitely didn't feel like talking. He asked in Spanish, "Is it alright if we sit with you for a minute?"

The boy didn't respond and Dale wondered if his grammar had been clear. The boy was in the swing furthest from the street, rocking very slightly. Under each of the swings, the sand was scooped out, filled with pools of shadow. Hoa took the first swing and Dale the middle one. He asked the boy where his parents were, where the townspeople had gone, and the boy kept silent.

This is like the Twilight Zone, Dale thought. The people of the town go missing. The single remaining child is mute.

"La iglesia," the boy answered politely in an impossibly quiet voice, looking at his sneakers.

"¿Son Americanos?"

"Si, somos," Hoa answered.

Dale asked in Spanish, "Is it some kind of festival?"

"No es un festival," the boy answered.

"What then?" Dale asked. Hoa got out of her seat and stood behind the boy as though she were going to give him a push in his swing.

Dale caught her eyes over the boy's shoulder.

"Es para Clarita," the boy said.

Hoa heard the name Clarita. She wanted to try her Spanish but couldn't formulate her syntax before the boy spoke again.

He said, "Ella se perdió en el desierto."

"What did he say?" Hoa asked.

"She got lost in the desert. Just a second," Dale turned back to the boy. "That's terrible," he said.

The boy was quiet, pushing back just far enough so that his shoes came off the ground, and then as he swung forward, stopping himself with his toes. Barely perceptible puffs of dust stirred up into the twilight's open mouth. The boy looked straight ahead as though he were in conversation with someone else.

Behind him, Hoa felt suspended between movements, disconnected.

Maybe the boy wanted to talk, Dale thought, keeping himself from blurting out the obvious question. He hoped Hoa would hold back too and give the boy time. Small bats whickered above them. The music from the barbecoa was imperceptible now and the multitude of stars had begun to press more distinctly into view.

"La encontraron esta mañana."

"So. Where was she?"

"Intentó hacer una pared con piedras."

Hoa walked to the side of the swings, resting her hand on the scuffed frame. The Spanish was too hard for her.

"I'm going to stretch my legs," she said. "I'll be back in a few minutes."

Dale tried to read her eyes before she turned away. Did she want him to come with her? Would she be pissed if he stayed? Had he taken over a conversation she had initiated? The boy waited quietly, until Hoa closed the gate behind her. She hesitated on the other side of the wall in the moonlight as though she were reconsidering. Then she started up the sidewalk, glancing once toward Dale. If she were sending him a message, a sign of some kind, Dale couldn't read it. He thought she would be fine on her own for a few minutes, and now he wanted to stay to hear the boy out. He turned back to the boy and asked why the girl would want to make a stone wall in the desert.

The boy went on then in Spanish, gradually growing more animated. "My uncle took us out to his ranch. We were sitting and bouncing on the balls in the back of his truck," he said.

"Your uncle keeps balls in the back of his truck?"

"Soccer balls. But the motor stopped and we had to walk all the way back."

"Did you have to walk far?"

"Muy largo. The road goes like this to the barranca."

The boy was making eye contact now, although it was too dark to see his face clearly. He looked somber, formal, but he spoke in bursts like he wanted to get something out. His hand dipped and rose in the air with the arc of a swallow.

"Clarita, she wanted to go straight across the barranca. But it was steep and Uncle was carrying little Miguel. So he said Clarita could take the shortcut and we would meet her on the other side."

"But when you got to the other side of the barranca, Clarita wasn't there?"

"We called and called, but she didn't answer. Uncle he was running back and forth, shouting and shouting. He scared me, his head scared me."

Dale didn't get that. Scared of his uncle's head?

"When he came back to the trees for us, he said we had to go on. Nobody talked the whole way. We just walked. Miguel was crying, but Uncle wouldn't stop. His head was hurting him. And when we came to Señor Urrutia's ranch, it was late."

"It took you until night to get back?"

"Señor Urrutia brought us home. My mother was crying in the kitchen. I went to bed, but my father woke me and carried me outside in the dark. There were four trucks by our house and men in them and we all came back to the desert. We parked right by the trees at the barranca. It was morning then and the men were arguing. They went in different directions calling for Clarita. I walked with my father. We climbed down into the barranca to find her."

"So it was a big search party."

"It was." He stared down at his shoes. The moon was swallowed by cloud. Wearing dark pants and a white shirt, the boy was dressed for church. In his face, only his teeth were visible in the dark. Following his lead, Dale looked down under his own swing at the drag pit in the sand. Just as he looked up again, something enormous swooped through the air ten feet in front of the swing set, a dark-luminating black mass that lifted into the pine tree at the edge of the park. The boy had seen it too. Denser than the darkness, like a floating negative space.

"Búho," the boy said. "Es un búho."

"Yes." Now Dale could make out its horned profile against the sky. "Yes, it is."

Still looking at the owl on its branch, he asked the boy, "Clarita, how old was she?"

"We're the same age."

"And you?"

"Nine."

"And why aren't you with your parents in church?"

The boy might have hunched his shoulders. In the shadow of the park, Dale tried to think of what to say. The owl let out four long morbid hoots.

"Nobody even found her. Only they found some of her clothes. And a pile of rocks where she tried to make a wall."

"Why was she making a wall?"

"For the coyotes," the boy said. "But the coyotes took her."

*six*

*And falls and falls*


Boy and man nearly naked
in the surf, excessively
incarnate, arms sprung out
from their sides, each
aware of the other intent
on the approaching waves.
From where she stands
wrapped in towel, windblown
sand pricking her calves, she sees
alertness in their shoulders
and necks as they bob forward
lithe as boxers and duck under
and are gone and come bursting up
at the same moment in a search
for one another. Let loose, what
belonged to her.

*Zona de Silencio*

Sliding his sunglasses onto the dashboard, Dale reached for the hood release, pulled it, and then opened his door into the epidemic of heat.

"Jesus," he said, turning his head so the word was directed back into the car as he unfolded himself from his seat and stepped out onto the shard-strewn dirt. It wasn't the sun so much as the dry air that made him blink. He instinctually started to close his door, caught himself, and left it open. With the doors shut and the engine off, the interior of the car would become a convection oven.

"I thought it was dust. Or a mirage." He was shading his eyes with the flat of his hand and surveying the desert, talking loud enough so that Hoa, still in the car, could hear him. "I'd been watching it blow over the hood, but it didn't sink in. What it was. What I was looking at."

In the torpid late afternoon, a nearly invisible steam was venting from the grill and from the seam all the way around the hood. Dale squatted in front of the car and poked his hand under the hood, feeling for the latch.

From the passenger seat, Hoa saw him crouch, then reel back like he'd been bitten. She'd been looking at the Google Earth printouts Dale had made of Coahuila, trying to track the shortcut they'd taken from Sierra Mojada west toward Jiménez. Now she threw them to the floor, opened her door, and got out. She, too, left the door open and skirted a brown puddle that was branching, amoeba-like, in the pebbled dirt by the front tire.

"Fucking scorcher," Dale said. He was squatting and reaching for the latch again, but he still hadn't opened the hood.

"Smells like sorghum," she answered. Her voice was flat, with a little surprise in it.

Dale hadn't noticed it before, but when she mentioned it, he thought he could smell the sweetness of cooked engine coolant.

"I can't get the hood yet." He stood up again, wiping his hands.

He's saying something just to say something, she thought. To show me he isn't scared. Which means this is really bad.

Dale took a few steps back from the radiant heat of the engine, tucking his burned fingers into his already damp left armpit.

"I don't know. I figured . . ." He didn't know what to say he figured. "I should have stopped way back there."

"This is incredible," Hoa said quietly. She pushed her sunglasses up over her forehead into her hair. She'd left the fedora in the car. With her sunglasses off and the recent tanning around her cheeks, the flesh around her eyes looked vulnerable and moist. She lowered her sunglasses again. On her side of the trail, the setting sun gilded the brush on the upper flank of what had once been a volcano. The formation peaked several hundred yards above the trail in half a dozen pinnacles of rust-colored rock. Most of the escarpment was sprinkled with creosote, ocotillo, and yucca. The brush was densest just in front of Hoa, a chest-high barricade on each side of the trail. Afternoon shadow was spreading along the hills toward them.

On the downslope side of the trail, Dale stepped close enough to the steep edge to peer through tall stalks of orange-flowered lechuguilla into a valley, a sunnied-over desert stretching to the south. An extensive plain hemmed by dark mountains. Hard to judge the distance, but the mountains looked far off.

In the direction the car was headed, the sky was lustrous and amaranth-pink. Hoa noticed the sunset and said to herself that it was a good sign. At least they knew they were facing the right way. West.

Dale looked behind him, where Hoa was looking. She's worried about the night coming on, he thought.

"So what's going to happen when they find out we took a rental car into Mexico?" she asked.

"They're not supposed to rent cars that overheat. Luckily—" he paused, groping to come up with anything that might seem lucky about their circumstance, "it's not mid-afternoon. So we might get the car started when it cools down a little. We'll get it back one way or another."

"We can't afford to pay for a lost rental car," she said, as though finishing Dale's thought.

They stood for a minute, not saying anything more—he in front of the car and she at the side where a foot-high berm of soft dirt, dotted with stones, marked the edge of the trail. Over a low-pitched gurgling, she could hear steam quietly hissing out from beneath the hood. Even now, in the late afternoon, the sun's rays were gnawing at her—not in one particular place, but everywhere, her head, face, neck, arms, shoulders.

"Yeah, lucky for us," she said.

She glanced at her watch, even though she knew the time. Her body always told her when it was around five o'clock. Pavlovian conditioning. Time for a glass of wine, time to think about making dinner. She remembered the bottle of tequila in the cooler.

"What about the water from the ice in the cooler?" she blurted. "Couldn't we use that?"

The way her voice lifted, he couldn't tell whether there was panic or excitement in it. Probably both.

"Great," he said, trying to sound calm and reasonable. He saw himself from outside himself: a man standing by the side of the road in the middle of nowhere with the hood of his car up. An icon of failed presumptions.

"Good idea," he said starting to move, calculating how much water there might be in the cooler.

The ice from the hotel in Monclova, how many scoops had she put in there? Water slapped the sides as he pulled the little blue and white Playmate across the back seat. He thumbed the release button and slid back the top. Maybe half an inch, a pint or two, sloshing against the bottle of Tres Generaciones Añejo tequila.

Leaning in from the other side, Hoa was reading his face for an assessment, feeling a last trace of the car's conditioned air slip past her cheeks.

"Maybe," he said, glancing across the seat at her face. Considering their predicament, it was weird that he noticed her cleavage through the loose top of her blouse.

"Might be enough to get us puttering down the road anyway," he said.

He reached into his pocket for his cell phone and turned it on. Searching, searching. He knew there wouldn't be a signal, but he had to check. Nothing. Zona de Silencio.

Now Hoa was sitting in the front seat, extracting her own cell phone from the console port. "We haven't passed a single car. Not a single one. In what, like two hours?"

From the edges of the car's hood, steam wisped upward.

"It's not going to work here," Dale said.

"Thing is," she answered, "we should have seen signs to Laguna de Ventura or La Perla a long time ago. According to these stupid maps. We should have hit 67 by now."

Dale returned to the front of the car and eyed the front grill logo, a blue cross. The engine had stopped hissing for the most part. Maybe that was good. Maybe it meant they hadn't lost too much water. Or maybe it meant there wasn't any more. Hoa came over and stood next to him, putting her hands on the back of her head and lifting her hair from the sweaty back of her neck.

"This is fucked Dale," she said.

She dragged her hands through her hair, gathered and twisted it into a knot, sliding the bungee from her wrist over it.

\* \* \*

"No holes anywhere," he spoke loudly into the engine. He was leaning over the still-ticking radiator, squeezing the hot black hose that led to the thermostat housing. "Could be the water pump. Could be the gasket's shot. Or maybe the thermostat."

"What about duct tape?"

His head turned in her direction and he straightened his back and looked at her incredulously where she was sitting in some soft sand, shading her eyes with her hand.

She saw the look in his eyes. "Maybe there's some in the trunk," she said defensively. "If there's a hole in the hose."

Dale changed tack. "You can check. There's nothing but a spare tire. And our duffel bags."

"So let's look," she said.

His hands were already filthy, but he fished the keys from his cargo pants and opened the trunk. He pulled out their two duffle bags and set them in the dirt. He lifted the mat, the flap underneath it. There wasn't even a full-size tire.

"I remember reading that you can plug leaks in a radiator with peppercorns," he said.

He went around to her side of the car and squatted down, grabbing the maps from the floor.

"Okay," she said, squatting beside him. "What are we going to do?"

"We should have rented a pickup," he said. "If we can't get it started, I think we should walk on. Toward La Perla and route 67. It's got be closer than going back to Sierra Mojada. Or maybe I should run ahead." He thought about that for a second. What would *she* do while he ran ahead? "Either way, we can't do anything tonight. Not on these fucking forking goat trails in the dark. We can sleep in the car and start early morning."

"What if this stupid trail doesn't go to the highway. Or anywhere."

Dale walked back to the front of the car and looked into the engine, taking his time with her question. The radiator was going to need to cool some more before he tried to restart the car. Hoa came up behind him ominously, waiting there, not saying anything, not touching him. He stepped to the side and surveyed the way they'd come. It wasn't much of a trail, just tire tracks bordered on both sides by stubby branches that had scraped the car's sides. Snippets of the trail were visible as it rose and fell through the knolls behind them. He thought, you look at the desert and it seems absolutely still. And then you look again and every centimeter is vibrating. Some flicker of movement drew his attention toward his left boot. A nacreous beetle scuttered out from the car. The sunlight hit it, and it reversed direction and disappeared under the car again.

"We stuck to the main trail all the way, so far," he said slowly, thinking it through, studying the coolant-stained dirt under the engine. "We went through two gates. And crossed maybe three, four cattle guards." He was just processing facts, but facts are stabilizing, he told himself. "If the trail keeps going west, southwest, it's going to link up to the highway. It has to."

"No," she said.

He had been avoiding looking at her face, but now he did. She wasn't contradicting him. It was an *Oh no this isn't happening* kind of no.

"This was such a bad idea," she said in an undertone. "Your shortcut. We don't even know if we're on the main trail, it's nothing but a dirt path. It's just a trace. You can't even tell if anything has come through here in months."

Panic. It was panic in her voice.

"We both looked at the maps," he said, thinking *you're the one who couldn't stand being in the car, who made me take the shortcut.* Deliberate. Making himself sound calm.

She knew he was begging her: *Don't blame me for this.*

"I asked those guys in Hercules," he said. "It looked pretty straightforward on the map. But Hoa, even if we lose a day. Even if we lose a whole day here, we'll be back sooner than if we'd driven back east all the way through Piedras Negras."

"I can't believe this."

Dale was surveying the darkening hill behind her. "I wouldn't mind seeing some goats," he said. "Or cattle."

A yellow jacket appeared from nowhere, hovering in front of Hoa's face, and she backed up, swatting at it. Then she fell backward on the berm at the edge of the trail. She covered her face with her hands.

That scared him. Then he was right beside her, on his knee. To some stranger happening by, it might look as if he were proposing. "Hoa, Hoa." He was trying just to get her to look at him, drawing out her name, her familiar name. He started talking quickly and softly. Assuring her that their lives weren't at risk. That she was frustrated, of course she was frustrated, and part of that was just all the damn driving. "We're going to lose a day. And we'll be okay. A rental's supposed to be in perfect shape. You don't want to blame this on me, that the car overheated." His brow was awash with sweat. He held out his hands black with engine smut. "I'm hotter and at least as frustrated as you."

He sat down next to her on the apron of the trail, as though it were natural that they would be sitting and talking on the side of two tire ruts running through an endless desert.

"It's not even a road," she said, sitting forward, gulping air, clutching at her trembling knees.

Then she pushed herself up suddenly, ignoring him. She went around the front door and slid into the passenger seat. What's she looking for, he wondered just as she popped out again and stalked to the back of the car to stare into the still-open trunk. There was nowhere to escape the heat. They would get out of this, he was thinking. Really, they had to be close to route 67.

They'd driven north from Sierra Mojada on a road so powdery, Dale used up most of the wiper fluid washing the windshield. The view from the inside of the car had become streaked in brown arcs and, in the corners where the wipers didn't reach, the glass was browned out.

The bad road from Sierra Mojada turned into something far worse: twenty miles of brutal sandy track, the car wheels locked into furrows on either side of a rocky hump. They had crawled north through a break between mountains into the mining town of Hercules, where they stopped for empanadas at a comedor. Crescents of iron rebar separated the weedless dirt from the swept concrete sidewalk before the doors of the eatery. Late for lunch, early for dinner, they had shared the dining room only with a pair of miners, each wearing a blue company cap.

On the way out, Dale asked directions, and Hoa heard one of the miners say, as the other nodded, "Al oeste en el camino de tierra, derecho derecho derecho." No mention of any forks or turns.

Now, Dale felt dread spilling out into the air around them. He went over to the trunk and tried to give her a hug, but she turned away from him and looked down the trail. He wondered if he should run ahead for a while, before it got too dark, to see if there were any hopeful signs. He reached into the driver's side and grabbed his sunglasses from the dash. Then he changed his mind and put them back.

"I'll check the belts. Soon as it cools off, we can put in the water from the cooler and we'll keep the AC off and the windows down and we'll putter on to the highway."

Putter? Hadn't he used that word a few minutes earlier?

Dale squatted at the driver's side tire, unscrewed the cap on the valve, and pressed the pin with his fingernail to bleed a little air. He felt Hoa looking at him and he quickly said over the hiss, "It'll ride better on the dirt." Going around to each tire and listening for the same length of hiss gave him something to do while the engine cooled. He couldn't see Hoa's eyes behind her sunglasses, but she had put on her fedora, stepped into a rut mark in front of the car, and was gazing across the desert. He screwed on the last stem nozzle and stood up, following the trajectory of her gaze. The evening was sinking into crevices in the outlying mountains, making them look like fists, one beside the other, thick, broken fingers clutching the earth.

If they abandoned the car, the ridge behind them would offer some immediate shade—if they fought their way through the bushes. He noted, here and there on the slope, a low mesquite tree or some kind of white-flowering bush, maybe cat's claw. From somewhere close, a mockingbird whistled a short repertoire. *Zenzontles.* The word came to him. That's what Mexicans called mockingbirds.

*Breakdown*

Neither of the two main belts that Dale could see in the early evening light seemed particularly loose. He pressed and poked at both of them. He hadn't worked on his own car since college and the Prizm engine was a new world. He ran his fingers along the ridge below the water-pump belt, thinking, What am I going to do if I find something wrong anyway? I don't even have a screwdriver.

He knew they were stuck there for the night, but he thought he might as well look engaged. If they started walking now, the dark would catch them, and there was really no telling where they were. Zona de Silencio.

"Xái tháng chó đẻ," he heard Hoa say, coming toward him carrying the Playmate cooler, with a harried, earnest look. Dale was focused on her face and didn't realize she was trying to figure out whether to hand the cooler to him or to set it down. By the time his body moved, the cooler was on the ground.

"Thanks," he said.

Dale hunched over it and slid the top back. She had already fished out the tequila. Alright, he thought. One chance at this. The empty coolant reservoir was on the driver's side. He wondered whether it would be better to pour the water into the reservoir or directly into the radiator. Pulling off his T-shirt, he balled it over the radiator cap and gave it a tentative twist. There was no hissing. He didn't feel any pressure. He twisted the cap all the way off and set it very intentionally on the dirty air-filter cover. Then he wiped his face with the shirt and pulled it back on. Keeping it slow, relaxed.

Hoa said nothing, standing aside while he tipped the cooler and poured the water carefully, carefully, into the radiator. It was obvious to both of them that there was far more coolant pooled and evaporating in the dirt than there was water to replace it with.

"Let's wait a few more minutes and then start it," he said.

Hoa was already behind the car, lugging the duffel bags from the dirt onto the back seat. Dale stood to the side and watched her rifling through them. The shirts and socks and underwear they'd worn yesterday, his running shoes and shorts. All their toiletries crammed into eight-ounce plastic bags for airport security. She had spread everything around the back seat and the floor like an augury.

Dale sat sideways behind the steering wheel, his back to her.

"Looking for anything in particular?"

She peered up. The effort of twisting in his seat to see her behind him made his brow furrow. She saw his reddened face and neck wrinkle into turkey folds. He looked suddenly old to her.

A tube of hair gel, a blue razor, his deodorant, his running watch, her face cream. "I don't know," she said. She tossed her fedora, a short-sleeved white blouse she'd worn in El Paso, and her tie-front blouse into the front seat. They slid onto the floor. Even with its doors open, the car seemed to be collecting heat. Dale lifted his feet to the chassis edge and observed a nopale cactus at the side of the road. It did nothing. The seat fabric was marked with his sweat.

"Will you pass me my dirty shirt and the tequila? I need to wash this crap off my hands."

"Here."

Dale put the shirt in his lap and held the tequila in his hand, reading the label. Then he broke the black seal and unseated the cork, pressing his balled-up shirt to the mouth of the bottle and tipping it three times. He reinserted the cork and put the bottle between his legs, wiping each of his fingers with the tequila-dampened shirt. Then he pulled the cork again.

In the back seat, Hoa sat with the duffel bags and the mess all around her. Dale felt her eyes on him, watching him take a sip. And then another. A sunbeam fell across his knees and hands. His wedding band gleamed.

* * *

Hoa moved to the front seat. She was glancing at Dale, glancing at the keys in the ignition, waiting for him to turn the key and try to start the car. She forced herself to turn away, to look out the open door. Which is when Dale turned the key one notch. The battery lights came on, and he powered down all the windows, turning the radio and the air conditioner off. Then he turned the key another click and then another, and the car started. They looked at each other, Hoa's eyes glistening. The engine sounded normal. Dale leaped out to close the hood and the back door. When she saw what he was doing, she jumped out and slammed the other back door.

Neither of them said a word. Both were sitting up stiffly, looking straight through the windshield as though the intensity of their concentration might help propel the car forward. The trail in front of them was darkening, losing its color even as the sky ahead of them roiled in magentas, purples, and deeper blues.

Dale shifted the car into gear and felt the tires snap into the sandy track. The steering wheel revolved under his hands as the wheels locked into the ruts, and they were moving forward. There was no guarantee the trail wouldn't just keep going until it petered out in the middle of nowhere. The miners at the comedor had told him to follow the main trail, but at some of the forks, there was no way to distinguish a difference. He was glad he'd let air out of the tires. The traction felt better.

Almost immediately, the coolant icon—an aquarium shape with low black waves—began flashing in the instrument panel. Dale quickly looked up through the windshield again. There was no point in letting Hoa know. He felt his internal organs deflate, and he suppressed a sob. Before they had gone a quarter mile, the temperature indicator spiked into the red zone. The way the steering wheel was adjusted, he hadn't noticed the temperature gauge. But now, with the tension in his stomach drawing him forward toward the dashboard, there it was. Emphatic as a rattlesnake. Dale glanced at Hoa. Her eyes were drilled ahead at the rocks and clumps of weeds between the trail's ruts. He debated turning on the headlights and decided to wait.

They slowly climbed a pitted, sandy slope, the undercarriage scraping, a vertigo-inducing drop-off on Dale's left. They could have jogged faster than they were moving. Parts of the trail were washed out, and he aimed the tires around the worst of them. At the ridge of a small hill, they saw miles of darkening cacti and creosote-studded desert, a stupendous view that went on for countless miles. The sky was kaleidoscopic. Giant. Blueing. At the southern horizon sat a black pile of rock.

Dale had driven only a minute or two along a ledge beyond the rise when the car needed more pedal to keep going at all. Then his right foot was to the floorboard and the car was slowing to a stop. The engine cut. In all, they hadn't driven fifteen minutes from where they first broke down. A long breath, and neither of them moved.

* * *

They got out one at a time, not because there was anything to do. There just wasn't any point in sitting in the car. On the passenger side, the trail was banked against a sandstone outcrop with blocky horizontal layers in various shades of umber. Dale considered it. If he scaled about twenty feet of rock, he would reach the upper part of the hill—where century plants were spiking the evening light—and he could scout ahead. He eyed the rock face, identifying a narrow, angled ledge that looked to hold him.

"I'm going to check up here," he said.

He went past her. She might have turned to watch him, but he wasn't sure. He stepped up to the wall of sandstone and got a foothold, gripping the rock above him with his hand. He was trying to remember if there were tarantulas in the Chihuahua Desert. He leaned his chest into the rock and balanced, stepping up incrementally until he made the lip, and then he stood on the hill. Fluff grass, cacti, yucca, mesquite. He jogged around the plants until he stood at the hill's apex. A light breeze brushed his cheeks, and he felt almost good, with the panorama slung out far in front of him. A taste of limitlessness. And then what he felt sharpened into grotesque awe. There was not a human sign anywhere. Nowhere below or ahead could he see the trace of a road. No ranches, no mining operations. He saw yardangs beyond yardangs. There was a monstrous canyon to the north with side canyons and tawny battlements, its pink chimneys fading pale. The skyline was blueblack. Dale struck out a hundred yards to the west. Just ahead, the trail disappeared, spooling around a hillock. It wasn't a breeze he felt at all, he thought. It was the suck of emptiness. The tiny damp hairs of his forearms stood at attention.

Hoa wasn't looking as Dale cat-walked back down the narrow ledge to the trail, his face to the rock. So she didn't see the thin ledge crumble under his step or see him spill backward into the trough of riprap beside the trail. What she heard was his shout of surprise and the rattle of falling stones and she rushed over, wordless, with fresh panic. There, twenty yards behind the car, Dale was lying on his side and gripping his ankle. Shaking. Or was he crying?

## The Tall Boy

A pony stands in traces on the street beside the central plaza. The jacaranda trees are fully leaved and raucous with grackles. Paths from each corner of the plaza lead past tented stalls to a garden of oleander, bottlebrush, and raked dirt. A balloon-shaped man tows a bouquet of colored balloons. Men old enough to have grandchildren stand hunched at bootblack stations with their eyes downcast, their thick fingers stained dark as their eyes, while barely school-age boys haul their wooden shoeshine kits on lopsided shoulders and scan couples strolling the paths, sizing up potential customers.

It is about five o'clock when a broad-shouldered man carrying a soccer ball approaches a bench where an old Maya woman sits, her eyes vacant. He takes off his white hat and places it carefully on the slats of the bench. Then he drops the ball beside the bench and kicks it to life, dancing a little, subtly, not drawing too much attention to himself, but deft, absorbed with the ball. He is a grown man but his knees are limber and his eyes focused. He catches the ball on the toe of his right boot, kicks it twice, three times, gently lets it drop, then bounces it forward with his heel. He stops the ball with his toe. A pair of teenage boys on their way somewhere pause to inspect him. Without seeming to notice them, he kicks the ball directly to the taller boy, the one with a thin mustache.

The street vendor squeezing lime over a roasted ear of corn observes the two boys and the man. One of the boys is holding the soccer ball now. The vendor cuts his eyes to ask his customer something and then sprinkles brown chile powder from a sandwich bag onto the corn. When he looks up again, the boys and the man and the soccer ball have disappeared. Instinctively, he glances toward the church. A clean, blue Dodge pickup truck starts up and pulls away from the end of the street. The two boys are seated in the bed. They are laughing and cursing and looking backward at the corn vendor and the diminishing plaza.

## Tres Generaciones

A huge cacophony of noise surrounded them. Where had the insects come from? There had been no bugs in the daylight—just a few wasps, he remembered, or yellow jackets, or whatever they were. Now there were thousands of creatures scratching out the sonic frequencies of their species in this ultra-night, each chirp and whirr distinct as a fingerprint. Having cranked back his seat as far as possible, Dale lay, looking up at the car ceiling and listening. With her feet just beneath his headrest, Hoa was stretched across the back seat.

Something like a floating spiderweb tickled his nose and he brushed it away. Maybe it was just a stray hair. Tomorrow and tomorrow and tomorrow. It would be a memorable day, one way or another. A snake-tongue of cooler air flicked in through the window. Black air. The din was impressive. The tequila was only a quarter gone. Dale found himself able to isolate individual calls from the palimpsest of sounds. A pair of owls hooting from somewhere along the driver's side hill. An electronic ticking—maybe cicadas—that gradually ratcheted into an anxious blender whine and fell off again. Loops and variations of this sound extended into the distances. The bleating of what—was it some kind of toad?

What had the waitress called it, toad with a sack? Then there was the infrequent, far-off yapping of . . . coyotes? Something nearby hissed in pulses like a grass trimmer. And now and again, he could make out the chirps of bats.

Behind him, Hoa shifted around, her face to the back seat. She was curled into a near fetal position. She had insisted she could sleep better there than in the reclined front seat. She had a point. He knew he would never fall asleep lying on his back like this. Even drunk. He probably hadn't fallen asleep on his back since he was a baby. They were both grappling around for position with their seats, but the seats were winning.

Dale wiped at his nose again, catching a whiff of his own grunge. An alien scent this time. If mosquitoes found them tonight, they were in trouble. But as far as he knew, there weren't mosquitoes in this part of the desert except maybe near standing water, which was rare, or near a ranch with cattle troughs. Actually, if mosquitoes bit them, it would mean water or people were nearby.

Dale pivoted his head to look out the side window. What incredible stars. Her eyes are probably closed, he thought. Earlier, he had heard her doing yoga breathing exercises.

He had to struggle to sit up and reach for the bottle in the passenger seat. He pulled the cork, took a swallow, and the burn went down his throat in two gulps. He put the bottle between his legs and reached for the ceiling light, twisting in his seat to check on her. The action felt cumbersome and the twisting put pressure on his face, making his eyes bug out and his sunburned forehead wrinkle. He couldn't see if her own eyes were closed, but she looked too uncomfortable to be asleep. Before he switched the overhead light off, he spotted a few gnats, or things smaller than gnats, crawling its plastic surface. A moth fluttered along the side of the windshield, sliding down to the wipers, remaining there.

Dale took another sip and contemplated raising his seat so he could sit more comfortably. He wasn't going to sleep anyway. The tequila was helping. They would probably walk by a ranch tomorrow before noon and get a lift to the highway and the nearest gas station. Worst case scenario, they would walk four or five hours all the way to the highway.

"Moon, moon," he quoted, "when you leave me alone all the darkness is an utter blackness."

She might have said something.

"What did you say?" he asked. Nothing.

He said, "I saw a beauty shop in El Paso called Hairway to Heaven. What's your favorite beauty shop name?"

No response. Then, softly, "The one makes me think of you. Hair Today Gone Tomorrow." Her voice sounded different to him when her eyes were closed, or when she was lying down.

"I know that one. In Franklin."

"Loose Ends," she said. Then, after a full minute and more faintly, she said "Curl Up and Dye for You."

Dale stayed quiet. He listened to Hoa's breathing change. Unsteady and shallow at first, and almost imperceptible, then gradually deeper. He could hear a kind of hollow vibration in her nose. The last thing he heard before he fell asleep was her stomach rumbling.

## Night Soliloquy

He woke twice needing to pee. The first time, he somehow remembered to turn off the overhead switch so when he opened the door, the ceiling light didn't wake Hoa. The second time, he took two hops on his good foot away from the car, but he lost his balance, and his bad foot touched the ground. The pain in his ankle cleared his head in a swoosh. As he tried to recover himself, he glimpsed something fluttering directly in front of him. A second shock paralyzed him before he even recognized what he was looking at.

It was a cartoon drawing, a dimensionless black nexus of thick lines. He'd never seen a spider so big, never imagined a tarantula lifting itself into a defensive posture, rearing back with its forelegs pawing the air like a tiny horse, quivering, waiting for him to make the next move. Some kind of yelping sound erupted from him. But he only heard it afterward, in a kind of echo loop, as he banged through the open car door into the steering wheel, toppling clumsily into the front seat against the dashboard.

"What?" Hoa snapped up in the back seat.

"Nothing, sorry, it's nothing." He had whacked his elbow on the door and his ear on the steering wheel. He was dizzy and out of breath and his ankle throbbed. "I just have to pee."

She stayed riveted in her sitting position. His door was still open. Now he gripped the steering wheel with one hand, planted his good foot on the rocker panel, and he extended his body from the open door to pee. His brain was woozy, cottoned with alcohol. Stupid, stupid. But considering his swollen ankle, his culpability for their situation, and the bottle of good tequila, well, he needed it. At least he had needed it a few hours ago. The night had been interminable.

He leaned from the door peeing in the general direction of the tarantula, then sat back in his seat, listening to the ratcheting of insects, the overlapping waves of sound, as he revised variations on ways to find help in the morning. Hoa was lying down again, mumbling something to herself or to him.

"You remember," he said in case she was awake, "you once told me a story you read in Ford Maddox Ford's memoir of Joseph Conrad? Remember that?"

Dale's voice was low now, his ankle settling down. He was talking himself calm, talking her calm. He went on quietly, not needing any response from her, looking through the windshield into the stars, audience enough. "How Conrad and Ford used to meet in England at some farm on a heath one of them was renting? They were collaborating on a book together is what you told me. And they'd go out on this heath just walking in big circles for an hour or so, and they were both famous talkers but Conrad was the really big one. I remember you said Conrad was kicking at the gorse. You used that word because I'd never heard anyone say it before—maybe I'd read it sometime and forgotten it. And you said Conrad was talking nonstop about his depression and his financial straits and about the Congo and how he had been poisoned by the Bomese, who locked him in a hut to die. But in the hut, there turned out to be all these old tins of condensed milk. And while Conrad is convulsing and dying, he gets the idea that maybe he should drink some of the condensed milk. He was just able to pierce the cans with a sharp stick and drink a few of them—only a master bullshitter could pass this one off—and of course, condensed milk turned out to be an antidote for the poison.

"I remember you said that Ford went on to describe Conrad. He said he was always quoting Flaubert and Maupassant, long passages, almost entire books, and commenting on the affairs of all these minor English politicians whose biographies he'd read and remembered. Conrad had an incredible memory and he would talk and talk, Ford not getting a word in edgewise. And the two of them would stop walking and stand still for a while and roll cigarettes and light them for each other, Conrad never letting up, telling stories a mile a minute. And Ford said that almost the whole time Conrad held forth in the field or the heath or wherever, he, Ford, was watching this pretty white-throated wren that seemed to be following them, hopping back and forth on low branches and then dropping to the grass or gorse or whatever to peck at something. And Ford—he's young enough to be Conrad's son and full of himself—sees himself as the great Modernist writer coming to save English literature. He thinks Conrad is too self-absorbed to register the barest detail of their surroundings. As far as Ford can tell, Conrad might as well be stem-winding at The Eagle Pub or in his living room as on the heath. But then, you told me, months later, Ford Maddox Ford opens a literary magazine and reads an account written by Conrad of that very outing on the heath, and the whole episode is just a showcase for Conrad's meticulous description of the antics of that white-throated wren.

"Anyway, that's what you told me. So I read the whole book, and when I finished, I went through it again backward, glancing at every single page, and I never came across the event you described. There's this great story Conrad tells about how when he first landed in England, some guy jumped out at him on the highway and shoved a volume of the English Bible into his hands, a pocket edition printed on rice paper. Conrad tore out pages and rolled his cigarettes in them for a month, but before he smoked, he always read the whole page, both sides, and that's where he got his first real feeling for the English language. And there's a memorable account of Conrad and Ford using an antique pistol to shoot rats in some abandoned granary—typically, Ford claims to pick one off at a ridiculous distance—but the part you told me about the two of them walking around talking and the wren, which is really even better, it's just not in there."

She had been breathing softly and regularly, with a tiny click at each inhalation, maybe she needed to blow her nose. He assumed she was sleeping. But she said in a flat natural voice, "No book's going to get us out of here."

174

*Friday Morning*

Daylight came and Hoa rose slowly into sitting position, her feet straddling the driveshaft hump on the floor. She reached into her purse, found her lens drops and squeezed some into her eyes, dabbing the runoff with her shirttail. Tired and stiff, she opened the back door. Last night she had been cool enough to rouse herself to try rolling up the windows. But they were electric and Dale had the keys in his pocket or somewhere. She had jostled his shoulder and called his name but by then—whenever that was, early this morning before any hint of light—he must have been in a stupor and didn't wake, so she lay back down and listened to a far off yipping she couldn't identify. Some cross between a small dog and a rooster. Now, she felt around on the floor for her Adidas and put them on, slung her purse over her neck and stepped outside into a becalmed world where she didn't belong.

A big sun hovered already above the horizon. The morning was warm but not yet hot. Don't worry about that, she thought. The heat's coming. She could hear her dread stirring inside her. It was as though one of the sun's myriad rays were dedicated to her alone, as though it had descended like the needle on a record player arm right onto her brain. And it was playing her thoughts, turning each groove of fearfulness into a sound only she could hear. She tried to get control of her flash panic, standing in the loose dirt, her back to the sun, consciously relaxing her shoulders. She looked down the trail ahead of the car. It was still there: the inhuman and more of the inhuman. Coming right at her like an avalanche of nada. She took a deep breath and let it out, joining her hands in front of her chest in the prayer position, trying to focus her energy.

The last peopled place they had passed was the little grit-blown mining town of Hercules. On the outskirts, they'd seen rubbled plateaus and enormous sinkholes. Identical houses looked onto ruler-straight streets while big, faded-yellow water trucks—Dale told her they called them *ranas*, frogs—sprayed water behind them onto the powdery road leading to the mine. They had driven west out of Hercules on a dirt road toward El Barreal. According to the map, they should have seen a lake on their right, Laguna de Ventura, but they never did. Going west and northwest, as they had, they should have hit route 67 just above La Perla after five or six hours. But the way forked over and over. They thumped across cattle guards, but saw no cattle. Hoa had to get out twice to open and close stick-and-wire gates. They had stuck to what they thought was the main trail, but it was impossible to tell.

If we keep going west, Hoa told herself, there's no way to avoid running into route 67. It may take awhile and we'll be thirsty, we'll be exhausted, but route 67 is west, that's a fact.

Already the sun forced her to raise her hand to her eyes to look across the desert to the spine of mountains in the south. Up above the ledge of limestone on her side of the trail, she saw cacti and a flowering yucca. It was only a little way further, but the vegetation was different here than where they first broke down. She squinted. The broken ledges of rock were soft, golden in the early sun. By the wall where Dale had fallen, she pulled down her pants and peed, and when she stood up again, buttoning the last of four buttons, she heard something close by. Big and very close, and she stopped dead.

Up on the hill where Dale had climbed last night, in profile, beside a dead ocotillo, a large black shape was pawing sand against its belly. It swung its enormous head toward her in slow motion. Wait, there were more! Behind the first, near a fat barrel cactus, a still larger animal was yawning. Hoa didn't move, she couldn't move, but she might as well have thrown a grenade, because the javelinas exploded, clattering up the hill and disappearing over the chine.

"Get up, Dale!" She was yanking open his door, but with the seat reclined, Dale's head was practically in the back seat.

"I'm up, I am up." He squirmed around in the seat, but seemed stymied as to how he might move himself into a vertical position.

"Get up. We've got to go." Hoa seemed to be looming in through the open door at him, retreating and then looming forward again. Dale found the lever for the seat, cranking himself into a sitting position behind the wheel. He needed to puke. What was in his mouth? His head stuffed with cotton, cotton soaked in formaldehyde. The gleam from the hood stabbed his eyes. Fuck!

"Give me the keys," Hoa said.

He leaned forward and took the keys from the ignition. Shit, Hoa thought. I could have turned on the battery and closed the windows last night. Reaching in, she pulled the half-empty bottle from between his legs. Turning, she threw the bottle as far as she could down the slope.

Dale wiped his eyes. The next thing he knew, Hoa was lifting the trunk lid, and he could hear her rummaging around again through the duffel bags. Do I need anything from mine, he wondered? He couldn't think what. His ankle was swollen and ached, and he struggled to reach down for his boots—no point in changing his socks—bringing one knee up from beneath the steering wheel. He tied the laces of his right boot very lightly. Both feet back on the floor. Now to orchestrate the act of getting out of the car. A gush of nausea started up in him.

Hoa slid into the back seat, leaving her door open. Prepped and ready. "We should start," she said again. "Let's get out of here."

"Give me a chance, I feel sick," he said. "Let me have the keys back for a second."

She reached forward, handing him the keys.

Dale didn't want to make a big deal about trying to start the car again. He put the key in the ignition. "You were talking in your sleep," he said. "You remember your dream?"

He turned the key. The dashboard light came on and the starter clicked, but didn't engage. Dale leaned back in the seat again. From the middle of the back seat, Hoa stared forward through the windshield. She did suddenly remember her dream.

"I was taken captive by these really bad people. They kidnapped children too."

"Why did they want you?"

"I don't know." She put her fedora on and looked at herself in the rearview mirror. "I wasn't my age in the dream. At some point, you were captive too, and you tried to escape on a skateboard going down a wall."

Dale looked to see where the sun was.

"I got away finally, but then there was a bear. Let's go."

Dale wanted to say something like "exit pursued by bear," but he couldn't muster the energy. In the rearview mirror he could see his own haggard face mottled by hangover.

"What happened with the bear?" he finally asked, trying to gain a minute.

"It was attacking a crowd, and then it skinnied up a big pole."

He tried to turn to look at her, wincing though he meant to grin. "We say *shimmied* in English."

"Shimmied. Let's go. It was a big thick pole and I knew it could climb up and down really fast."

"Were you on the pole?"

"No, come on, Dale."

"Then how come you were afraid of the bear?"

"I knew it would come after me."

"Why?"

"Because it was my dream, idiot."

*seven*

*Something*


As if iteration
might introduce us
to a sensation
not limited to sameness.
Which is when
the branchiomandibular
muscles contract
forcing forward the hyoid bones
in their sheath so
the woodpecker's
long tongue, forked
at the base of its throat and
wrapped over the top of its skull
and around the eye socket,
squirts through the drill hole
into a gallery of
insects within
the dead cactus.

## A Life Askance

Hoa had sunk deeper into the couch after they returned from their son's non-graduation. She thought about her boy, thought about her boy. She spent weeks putting together scrapbooks of his writing and she framed crayon pictures he had drawn in elementary school. Dale would come home from work and find her on the couch watching the Lifetime Channel, which he could identify by the sappy music and the ridiculously sentimental dialogue before he entered the room, no matter what movie was playing. They would take turns making miserable dinners for each other or picking up takeout. Otherwise, when they were home, Dale read or worked on his Ambrose Bierce book in the basement. When he got up in the night to go to the bathroom, he would turn off the light in the TV room and let Hoa go on sleeping on the couch. If the blanket had fallen, he'd cover her.

He assured her that, of course, Declan would get in touch again. That despite all the boy's anger and righteousness, he loved them. That it just might take awhile. "You weren't thinking about *your* mom in your twenties," he reminded her. "You weren't calling her all the time."

But she had never shunned her mother either. Argued with her, yes, constantly through her twenties and beyond. But she hadn't completely cut off contact with her. Her mother always had her phone number, knew where she was living. Hoa said, "We don't even know if Declan's safe. If I only knew that." Her eyes glassed over. "I have to know that."

Their son had returned to college after his release from the hospital only to drop out toward the end of his last semester. They didn't find out he was gone until they went up for graduation. They spoke to two of his teachers, one of whom said that their son was an unusually gifted young man. Argumentative, anti-authoritarian, serious, those words came up in every conversation. The professors had no idea where he'd gone. Neither did his former roommates, or they wouldn't say.

For months afterward, Hoa mechanically went to her studio, throwing ugly pots and smashing them back into shapeless clay. She'd come home in the late afternoons to sprawl on the couch with her books and anti-depressants. Dale would bring home prepared food from Whole Foods or the Thai place or Be-Bop Burrito, and they would eat on TV trays watching the news. In the evening, Hoa took her sleeping pills, and Dale took his anti-anxiety pill.

It took months, but gradually, Hoa began to come back to life. Wounded, yes. But she became increasingly functional. At Dale's suggestion, she started yoga classes—hot yoga even though it was summer. Dale would come home from teaching summer school and find her rimpled green yoga mat drying out on the back of a kitchen chair, and he would hang it up in the closet and come across it, the next day, on the kitchen chair again.

Long runs through the neighborhood helped him deal in his own way with his load of helplessness and guilt—whatever he had done or failed to do, whatever had brought on his son's anger, his silence, his disappearance. Dale would wake up long before the alarm, obsessing on moments like the time when he had been digging a hole in the backyard for a little pond and Declan had come out and asked if he could help. He had told him it was really a one-man job. Why had he said that? Why the hell? And then Dale would get out of bed and drink a protein shake and dress for a run. An hour later, enveloped in the regular sound of his own heavy breathing, half-hypnotized by the mantra of his shoes whap whapping the road as he paced between tents of gauzy streetlamp light past houses in which he knew everyone was still dreaming, his head would begin to clear. That was his time of communion with the world. In the concentrated quiet, all his senses became a listening, and he, a moving prayer.

## A Bad Case

Even more than water, Dale needed shade. He just needed to lie down for a while out of the sun. His insides cramped and his knees quivered now and again under him as he walked in a hop-along fashion, putting as little weight as possible on his bad ankle. Hoa marched ahead. For a while, Dale limped after her, putting one foot in front of the other along the dirt trail, each footstep expressing a thin puff of dust. His face down, he studied those puffs of dust over and over. When the sun briefly ducked behind the edge of a cloud, he felt more than saw the world change color around him and a thin hope was resurrected inside his fatigue. On his left side, scraggly cacti, acacia, and brush clamored to the edge of a deep drop. There was a flat stretch of desert below, and in the distance, rows of blue-green mountains.

He hadn't limped very far when a high, clear whistle drew his attention to his right. He steadied himself, shading his eyes with the flat of his hand, scanning the arrays of candalaria between him and the rise a few hundred feet away. One tall, yellow wand of yucca stood up from various collaborations of brown and green. Where the hill steepened, the brush and cacti thinned out, and a sill of naked rock erupted against flat blue sky. Like a ruined castle.

Dale could make out a band of quartz gleaming in the sill. The whistle repeated.

Dale didn't see the bird, but he thought he saw a bear hunched at the base of the massed rock. Weird, like from Hoa's dream. But it wasn't a bear, it was a dark opening, a cave. He would have never seen it if the bird hadn't called. It didn't look too far away. If he could climb up there, he could wait out the sun's assault and gather his strength. He stood on the trail like a scarecrow, dizzy, his puke-hollowed stomach vibrating, gurgling, while Hoa kept walking on. He was about ready to sit down in the trail. His tongue was like a shoe in his mouth. He tried to swallow, but could not. He wiped the sweat from his face, and his cheeks and nose stung with the grit on his fingers. He stood there, lifting the waist edge of his black T-shirt to his face, and it occurred to him that although he was dehydrated, he was still sweating profusely. His wrinkled organs were squeezing the last of their tinctures through his skin. He drew the wet back of his hand against his lips, felt the wetness but could not taste it.

Hoa was far ahead of him now. He took a moment to look around. Barren rock, desiccation, and emptiness everywhere. Just beside the trail, the brush was chest-high and thick, without a hint of an animal path or an opening. The sun buried its thorn into his skull. Dale looked back down the trail toward the car, barely visible now, less than a half mile away. Then he looked up the trail. Hoa had turned around and was coming back to him. Hoa to the rescue.

He waited for her, telling himself that he might recover himself more quickly in the cool of the cave. Remembering that miners had found a cave of giant crystals somewhere in Chihuahua. Rhomboid crystals bigger than school buses.

When she stood in front of him, he was startled by her eyes: all the different emotions there, like trees with birds shifting through them. Every muscle in her face was tense, and her plump lips had narrowed. He explained calmly that he was going to wait a few hours, rest his ankle, and then come after her. He saw her see the tears running along his nose and he wiped his temples and his stinging eyes. He said something about sweat. As he was wiping his cheek with his shirt, she put her arms around him, taking him by surprise.

While she held him, the bottom of his damp shirt caught up around his chest, she could feel his heart beating so wildly against her own that she felt joined by it and feared it might pry loose if either of them pulled away.

Dale was relieved that she agreed to go ahead without him. She'd stay on this trail and leave a sign for him if she turned at a fork. He would rest and catch up. He apologized as she kissed him quickly on his wet cheek. Hoa turned unsentimentally, but Dale put his hands on her shoulders, massaging her shoulders and neck while she stood waiting to be released into pure uncertainty. He worked his thumb down along her inner shoulder blade and heard that wonky ligament pop. Stepping in place like a toy soldier, Hoa said, "I'll see you soon," and she walked forward without turning her head, saying nothing more. Dale could see those hamstring muscles rounded against the back of her pants.

He watched her go, thinking she would look back but she didn't. Then he stared up at the cave. It was pure chance that he'd seen it. If they'd been driving, the cave mouth would have been imperceptible. Dale took a breath and projected a trajectory, glancing from the cave to Hoa to the cave. Then he plunged between two bushes, feeling the sharp branches scrape his arms and hearing them scratch loudly at his cargo pants. He was out of breath right away, slipping, almost fainting, losing any view as he stepped over dead palo verde branches, sidestepped cacti, and slowly worked his way around boulders. Because he had to concentrate on each step, he stopped every fifteen feet or so to look up toward the cave, to breathe deeply, and to take stock of his position. Instead of climbing directly, he had angled around to the right, where the candalaria and dwarf juniper—with its bark like alligator skin—was lower and less dense. The resinous scent of creosote rose as he forced his way through a phalanx of face-high shrubs, and the exertion actually seemed to reawaken his senses. That was a good sign. He could still smell. Under his boots, the loose talus clattered, and he lost his balance repeatedly, dropping down to one knee but not falling.

In his mind, he was calling out to the snakes, imploring them to let him pass—*Snake, snake, coming through snake*—but his lips weren't making the sounds. His open-mouthed panting, the brush clawing his clothes, and the sliding scree under his boots provided ample enough warning to snakes that he was coming. He pushed ahead and in his wake, vapor rose from the bushes he swiped. The distance was further than he had figured. The sun kept at him, and he felt his skin—the back of his neck, his arms, his scalp—cooking. Intense heat was radiating into his brain, reflecting onto him from all the scorched world. Dale thrashed along as if inside a cloud of fire, red pain pulsing behind his eyes, pouring out under his skull, throbbing and fading out in time to be replaced by a fresh set.

It took him half an hour to get close enough to realize there was an easier route—a sluiceway below the cave, only partially clotted with gnarled and twisted trees. When he came back down, that way would be the quicker going. Finally, he stepped clear of the line of brush, toward the jutting volcanic rock face, and he was able to peer up at the cave apprehensively. He was more afraid of the sun at this point than he was of a mountain lion. Still, it unnerved him to be so close to the cave without being able to see inside. The blackness he had spotted from the trail wasn't just the shadowy interior. The rock itself had been blackened by fires. Dale limped closer and saw that the cave was shallow, only about fifteen feet deep, high ceilinged at the opening, but quickly closing off. Then he saw there were dark crevices extending further back than he wanted to explore. The floor was covered with ash, through which a narrow footpath had been tramped. He stepped into the cave's mouth, into its blue shadow, and heaved himself down against the side wall, resting the back of his head against the stone. He stared out into the day, letting his exhaustion overtake him. Wondering how deranged his senses were, he thought he smelled something sweet and skunky and familiar before he coughed shallowly and passed out.

*The Firing*

At eleven p.m., Tuesday before her trip, Hoa met her firing partner, Veena, at Studio Clay Co-op. They passed through the gallery
space into the common room, its dusty tables strewn with sets of
pottery waiting to be glazed or painted—plates, dishes, vases, sake
cups. In the individual studios constellated around the common
room, sculptural work was drying under polyurethane sheets.
They exited the back of the building and let themselves through
the locked gate into the kiln complex, a fenced-in, weedy, open-air
acre of trees and sheds and piles of all sorts of things—stacked
pine and poplar, mill scraps, salvaged sewer caps. Over the kilns,
rudimentary tin roofs were pierced by tall chimneys.

Talking softly, Veena and Hoa walked through an inner courtyard, where six long clay-mixing tanks resembled eerie sarcophagi
in the moonlight. They ducked under the tin roof, stepping onto
the concrete platform of the kiln. It was a small downdraft style,
its door already bricked and mudded. A yellow electrical wire led
from a thermocouple inside the kiln to a pyrometer set up on a
dirty wooden stool.

Veena squatted and removed two bricks from the wall of the
ashpit below the kiln while Hoa went through two cribs of dry-

wood edgings. She picked a few of the thinnest ones and slid them across the concrete floor toward Veena, now leaning forward from her stool in front of the kiln. Veena placed the edgings over a bed of scrolled newspaper in the ashpit. She lit the paper, adjusting the wood in the flame. As it began to take, she tossed on strips of bark.

The fire rose from the ashpit through the grate into the firebox, and they continued to add thin wood. After two hours, the pyrometer registered 435 degrees, and Veena blocked the mouth to the ashpit with two bricks, opening the firebox door above the grate. Hoa shoved two-foot lengths of cut pine into the firebox.

Now the lengths of wood fell into a conflagration already roaring upward, and as Hoa added more split pine, it swelled the firebox, was sucked through two draft holes, and shot up along the interior kiln walls. Hoa kept adding edgings as the fire vaulted up to the cat arch where, given nowhere else to go, it turned downward into the center of the kiln, passing over shelves of clay pieces before it was siphoned out through a low exit damper in back.

Five hours after first lighting the crumpled newspaper, Hoa and Veena were moving with an incredible mutuality. Hoa lifted and slid the heavy iron door of the firebox and shoved four more thick staves and four thin ones into the crackling fire. With her mitted hand, she slid the door back and shut it again over the firebox mouth. Veena leaned against the wood stack, and Hoa sat on the stool in front of the kiln. Both turned their gazes toward the pyrometer. They were working smoothly as a team, like dancers alternating the lead, talking about slips and glazes, Veena's fiancé, common friends. Slapping mosquitoes.

Sliding aside the door again, Veena forced five thick and five thin lengths of wood into the firebox. One jammed, and she batted it with the butt of another until both fell into the flames. The wood crackled prophetically. She slid the heavy firebox door closed; they sat in silence as the temperature rose into the end of the stoke, and then Hoa took the pyrometer read. Pungent smoke circled up under the tin roof, mixing with the incense Hoa had set in clay balls on the floor to discourage mosquitos.

Veena arranged the next round of split wood upright against the side of the kiln.

"What have you been stoking?"

"My last one was five-five," Hoa answered, penciling notations in the record book.

Then they heard a different kind of crack from inside the kiln, and two more. Simultaneously, both of their bodies went rigid. Three muted clay explosions. Veena's eyes widened as they caught Hoa's.

"It isn't your piece," Hoa said.

She squeezed herself between the stack of wood and the side of the radiant kiln, reaching down carefully to take a brick from the side hole. On the other side of the kiln, Veena was doing the same.

Then both of them were standing shoulder to shoulder like mourners behind the stoking stool, looking at the pyrometer.

"I think it's mine," Hoa said. "The thickness was uneven."

"It's too late anyway," Veena answered.

Mosquitos swarmed them as the air went dead. The kiln blared its outrageous heat. Hoa put on her welder's goggles, stepping up on the stool to check the peephole.

"Maybe it was the clay wads," she said.

*A Vision*

There was an occasional pip from the mud nests glommed to the ceiling of the cave. Then when an adult swallow shot inside from the world of light, there was a choral explosion of cheeping. One of the nestlings fell from its mud cup into the spatter cone of bird-lime and broken eggshells on the rock floor. Dale was aware of this as he slept. Sometime later, he was aware of the injured chick stumping toward him, using its wings as props, its disproportionately large, naked head skewed to one side of the scrawny neck, dragging. It came on slower and slower until it stopped, near him, along the wall of the cave.

Dale could see with an incredible vividness through his eyelids. Now in the half-light, he watched a fly tamping around in the opaque eye of the dead chick. The fly was testing the inner edge of the eye with its foreleg, turning and dipping its bristled abdomen into the eyeball's seam. Then there were more flies on the bird's corpse. Surveying its head, walking the rim of the eye and beak, fussing and fusing with each other. And the dead bird's oversized eye was glazed with clots of eggs.

He thought, They'll know I'm dead before I know. The flies.

Above him, swallows swooped in and out through the cave

mouth, making pithy calls, *pwid, pwid*. Dale considered what they were saying, his mind weightless and clear above his body.

In the darkness of the wall to his left, Dale came to notice, without turning his head, a strange, patterned bulge, like a woven bag stuffed into a nook. He was beginning to be able to put his thirst away into a pocket of his dormant body, in order that he might observe the plight of everything animate and inanimate around him. I'll sit here a while longer, he thought. Until it's easier to breathe. His ankle was numb now. His whole body was numb.

Then the swallows went quiet.

Without moving his head, he swerved his eyes toward the bulge in the cave wall. It transfixed him. He could sense it pulsing, faintly glowing, its dark diamond patterns dimming and resetting in shadow. Two crickets deeper into the cave called and answered, answered and called. Was it night? Something was eating its way out of his own eye-pits. He could no longer see, but his mind worked like a radar system. He could perfectly track one cricket approaching the other. When they met against the rock, he could sense their antennal fencing.

He thought of Hoa walking ahead on the trail, walking alone toward the highway to get help. Then the heaviness of his body began to return to him. He struggled to find the way back to himself. She was alone and in trouble, and he could not help. He was useless as a horse on its side. She had added to his life, over and over, moments of recognition. As he stood up in her. As she swandived into him. All these years together, and everything he had learned about love before and during their marriage, he had learned in order to love her.

He recalled Hoa's peculiar knack for putting away anything he happened to be using when they were home. He would take down a wine glass, step around the counter, reach for a bottle of wine from the rack, and she would charge into the kitchen, put the wine glass back in the cabinet, and start talking to him about something. There might be a stack of dishes at the sink, but the only thing she would touch was the thing he had just set there to use.

And she was with him now, wherever else she was. Traces of her skin on his skin, her hair in his hair, her fluids in his body, all the wine and saliva and crumbs that had passed back and forth between their mouths innumerable nights, and words and each other's dreams. Hoa's dreams. Dale knew that he carried them inside himself, in his memory, even though they only ever existed as fugitive chemical trails in Hoa's brain, quick-fading memories she told him once and later forgot. They were among the most vivid of his intimacies with her, those dreams for which he had become a repository, her picaresque and silly dreams which he would forever carry.

Dale bored through the rock in front of him with his gaze. He was watching for Hoa to return across the flatness of desert. As soon as he knew that's what he was doing, he heard her, she became audible to him even before she was present. He heard her voice, the warm familiarity of her voice. The words weren't specific. And now he saw her coming toward him, a quivering figure imprinted in the throbbing air. He saw her twinned, coming at him along the dirt track, sometimes in one rut and sometimes in the other. Two of her. Then a shadow lifted and the human figures wrinkled, melting, and resolving into a single cactus a few dozen paces from the cave's mouth. It came no closer to the cave, although it broke again and again through shimmering veils of heat and light.

A general multilayered chirping filtered into a single, high, constant trill, a soft background sound into which occasional swallows tested their voices. And then the ratchet of a toad— Dale's old friend the pouched toad—a few bars of its corrido at a time. A moon was drawing up from the floor of the desert. Unburied lumen. In the upper arch of the cave's mouth, Dale caught the gleam of a spider's thread. He heard the thin chir of a bird outside. Then he heard Hoa's voice call it an elf owl. Through his closed eyes, he studied the early evening.

With her eyes closed, that was how Hoa danced. Like she was blind. Her elbows would lift outward, her hands dangling in front of her, her fingers spread, each reaching separately for the music as though someone had snatched away a keyboard she was still playing. They had neither one of them mastered any formal dance like the salsa or even the box step, and whenever they slow-danced, they would find themselves pulling in different directions. He tried to lead with determined regular rhythms but got bored quickly and would introduce a counterpoint or a whirl and one of them would stumble. He'd step on her toes. He'd pull her against him, then lean her back so far their dance shifted from the provocative into the salacious. But to a harder rock-and-roll beat, Hoa would sway like a cobra in front of him, unsighted, with her hands dangling like tendrils at her waist, and that itself was provocation enough for him to reach out to touch her as they danced, to let her feel his fingers brushing her belly, her thighs, the curve above her hip.

He sensed there was a rattlesnake in a nook of the cave wall, but he couldn't fix its position. The wall was a shifting kaleidoscope of darkness and darker darkness. Staring through his eyelids, he began to experience the balled snake in one place and then in another. Soon, the whole cave wall began to expand, to inhale, to nudge a little closer to him so he could see more of the rock's color—the iron coming out like a flush—and then he saw through the wall to the other side, to the sea of creosote and yucca flowing out across the desert. There, the landscape was a negative of itself, the air obsidian and the desert phosphorescent white. It was a gift, this vision. It was a glimpse he had been granted of the world through the snake's brain, a world rendered not by light but by the heat inside each thing.

A wobble in the atmosphere of the cave caused Dale to moan and draw his legs up under him. Gradually he came to know that he was surfacing, coming awake again. He felt his shoulders against the rock and leaned back for support. He was trying to stand. Slowly, slowly. A hobbled journey toward the vertical. A sharp pain flashed in his ankle. What was going on outside the cave in the late afternoon? Something. Some kind of inferno. Some excess in the desert's far appearance.

Once more he opened his eyes. His right shoulder knocked against rock and he was standing inside the mouth of the cave. He knew nothing but the blur of light and then a quivering that was also made of light. Lurching outside, barely keeping his balance, he saw, beyond the two-rut trail from which he had climbed, an expanse of desert sparkling and alive and real. A red-tailed hawk soared overhead. In the dreamy far-off, outlying ridges and skirts rose into sharp, naked peaks, with further ranges stacked behind them in shades of purple.

Dale looked at his hands, his filthy pants, his dusty, untied boots. He was sitting against the cave wall again, his eyes were open. He closed and opened them purposively. Hoa? He got himself to his feet again. Out in the desert, something was happening, a sight beyond his comprehension. He tried to blink the haze away. He concentrated on breathing in and out, in and out.

His eyes opened once more. He was upright, observing a luminous, gilded whirlwind in the desert flats beyond the trail. He watched, thinking: I am awake now, my ankle aches, my eyes are open, I am thirsty, my throat is swollen shut, I am standing with my weight on my left leg. Breathing in, breathing out. But was he awake? He wasn't certain. While he stared, other golden vortices began to form in the desert, until five of them, spectacular and tall, were stalking, circling each other like wrestlers. A carbonized setting sun embedded itself behind all the stormy drama. Then he understood that the air itself was sand, a tumultuous cloud of floating, crystalline sand. He reeled forward one more step, impressed by the vivid stab in his right ankle. Awake, yes I am. Two of the nearer whirlwinds approached each other, one tilted forward and the other bent back, their tops indistinct, merged with a strata of turbid haze. They jockeyed nearer and nearer, crossing the desert, and then in a violent convulsion, the whirlwinds seemed to grab hold of each other. It was impossible to tell whether they collided or merely passed so closely that one velocity countermanded the other. In the next moment, the two shapes staggered, trembled, and fizzled into a huge sigh of painterly shimmer that blurred the sun and darkened the desert. The remaining giant funnels continued on their separate ways in an erratic twilight. Dale dropped through one level of awareness into another and found himself sitting again, staring at his boots. He became conscious of his own shallow breathing and made an effort to take a bigger breath. He held it a little and let it out. Weed. *Mota.* That's what he smelled.

* * *

Veena put on her gloves and goggles, stood on the stool, and pulled the plug on the upper peephole. Between her gloved thumb and finger, the tip of the plug was cherry red. She kept her head back while a clear flame shot three inches out of the peephole.

At 1560 degrees, Hoa adjusted her infrared goggles and yanked open the firebox door, throwing in staves as fast as possible while the heat whelmed her chest and face. Five medium and five thin staves, one after the other, keeping heat loss to a minimum. The fire was the color of electric goldfish. When new staves met the flame, Hoa heard them crinkle and dissolve.

At 1650 degrees, a gaseous orange flame blasted from the peephole. The acrid, ashy smell began to give the stokers a high. The kiln temperature rose quickly now, so quickly the flame, needing more oxygen, began to suck it from the clay vessels themselves. When the pyrometer read 2010 degrees, Hoa eased herself between the stacked wood and the kiln to open the damper, the hair on her arms singed, and she emerged flushed, wiping sweat from her forehead. The solid kiln looked pregnant, its bricks expanding outward, smoke and light pouring from gaps where clay mortar had fallen away.

Veena was stoking six plus six, the wood meeting flame hissing like bacon in a frying pan. Between stokes, Hoa selected staves, setting them upright against the kiln on Veena's left. As Veena shoved one stave into the firebox, Hoa held out the next one. Then they switched places, Veena pulling the collar of her shirt up to wipe her glistening face. Hoa opened the firebox and used a stout piece of green wood to stir the ash over the grate, a sheet of smoke unwinding from the firebox and enveloping her.

Veena slid sideways between the kiln and the wall and tapped open the side damper another inch. She slid out and drained her water bottle in breathless gulps. In mutual exhaustion, both women sat on separate stools watching the pyrometer, waiting for the moment when the heat would stop rising and they would need to stoke again. In the open pit beneath the firebox, embers flared and shifted. Heat. Bring it on. Hoa could take the heat.

*Hoa's Walk*

The weekend before they left for Mexico, Dale had flown to DC to visit his parents. He had called her from a downtown bar, a little drunk, and it was hard to hear him over the bar noise. He was saying "I'm at this place called, believe it or not, Wisdom. With my sister. We had to get out of mom and dad's house. So we're drinking ginger mojitos. Here I'm standing at the bar and all I can think about is you. I can't be having a good time without wanting you with me."

She felt such tenderness inside her when he said that. Softly, she told him "I'm witchoo baby." She'd once heard Dale's Virginian cousin say it like that, and ever since, she and Dale would pass the phrase back and forth to each other. "Witchoo baby." "Witchoo too." But he hadn't heard her with all the bar noise.

Witch-you-babe-bee. Each step she took now seemed to deliver one syllable of that phrase. Over and over, as she walked the sandy rut of the trail. The flat-topped mountains off to the north were low enough to call hills or mesas. She could see bushes climbing the slope. It was beginning to darken with evening. Her feet were sweaty inside her shoes. Witch-you-babe-bee.

She spotted a single shining dragonfly wing stuck between two small stones in a berm. She noted two fluffy underfeathers in the dirt. A black skink, and later another one, fluttered across the trail and disappeared. Some kind of camouflaged grasshopper clung to branches of the chaparral.

I won't sleep, she told herself. I can walk through the night.

She felt the low angle of the sun on her cheek and thought about how it must be on Dale's cheek too. What was he doing? Was he limping along behind her? This same sun, this same sun. And her boy? What was he doing? The more she imagined Declan, letting herself think about his state of incommunicado, the more her breath shallowed as she walked. She felt as though her heart were sinking toward her solar plexus, drawing a draft of pure sadness after it. Not her own life, it wasn't her own life she would miss most if she never found her way out of this desert.

*eight*

## *The Iteration*

From the grooved highway at sixty-five,
a hum rises. Except intimacy
there is nada. That
was a scissortail the woman says.
The boy in the back seat stops
blowing his Coke bottle
as they pass
the mowing machines. Spiked
lobelia, crown vetch, trumpet vine
under the blades of the Ditch-witch tremble.
What is the true jelly of an animal?
asks the boy, tonguing his tooth
on its last string. The woman
turns her face smiling.
The skyline jumps over the moon.
The man drives with his finger
inside her. Years
of together. The theories
were unfit to live on.
Only dust was given duration.
They know that
they are naked.

Outside the cave, in the fading day, Dale stood teetering on the hill of talus. Quickly, he thought. He bent, going light-headed, and picked up a flat rock larger than his palm, limping with it to the closest nopale cactus. There were dozens of nopale dispersed in the slather of brush on the hill, and barrel cacti too, although they looked more formidable. The prickly pears on the nopale were green and orange, dotted with brown nubs anchoring displays of spines. The fallen fruit was desiccated and withered, and none looked edible. Dale dropped the rock by his boot, struggling out of his shirt. Bending forward to keep from going faint, he spread the black shirt on the sandy brash. *Before the light goes.* He picked up his rock, tapping at a ripe fruit. It detached instantly, falling onto his shirt. He knocked off six prickly pears, piling them together. Then he tested the edge of the rock against one of the green, flipper-like pads from which the fruit grew. The pad, too, dropped readily from the cactus. He limped back to the cave carrying the rock in one hand and his shirt, folded around the nopale pad and fruit, in the other.

Dale eased himself against the near wall where he could see in the dimming light. His senses beginning to revive. He scoured the back wall anxiously for the rattlesnake, but didn't find it. Against the blackness of the back wall, he did make out a man-sized passage of more profound blackness, a tall, skinny tunnel leading further into the cave. Leaving the open shirt of nopales, he tentatively crawled toward the passageway, the sharp rock floor chaffing his knees through his torn cargo pants, and he sniffed the skunky pungency. Somebody's stash.

Get out of here, he told himself. But the rental car was on the trail. Hoa, was she still walking ahead? Which way would they come from if they came? An adrenal rush lifted the hair at the back of his neck. He crawled back toward his shirt, trying to clear his head. Beyond thirsty. Strategizing frantically.

If the cave was situated halfway between Sierra Mojada and highway 67, the narcos might come from either direction. If they came from the highway, they would run into Hoa. Or not necessarily. There were several trails. They might come from Ciudad Camargo, farther south. Or they might come from Jiménez. But if they came west from Sierra Mojada, they would find the rental car on the trail less than a mile from the cave. Then again, the car was close enough that they would see it no matter how they approached. And the keys were in it.

In the flat light at the mouth of the cave, Dale studied the nopales spread out on his shirt. First this, he thought. This first. One thing at a time. He took his sharp-edged rock and mashed open a prickly pear on his shirt. It split on first impact, and he teased it further apart, pressing out the succulent wet green with its slimy nest of brown seeds. With his thumb and finger, he tweaked some and brought it to his face. His lips felt as though they had been sewn shut. His tongue was bulky in his mouth, and he could barely swallow. He sucked at his slimy fingers and rested. Then he smashed open two more, sloppily scooping the middles with his fingers. At first he couldn't taste the moistness, and then he could feel it inside his lips, reviving the aftertaste of his own sour puke. He gagged, but he bit down, keeping the gleet in his mouth. He sucked it around either side of his tongue and swallowed a little at a time. Electric jolts rippled his brain and dissipated again.

When there were no nopales left, he took up the rock and tapped at the flat green pad. It spurted onto the cave's floor, and he panged for the lost fluid. He pinned the pad with another stone and scraped back part of the skin. It was a mess. He was mucking it up. There was more pulp in the pad than in the pear, but it was hard to get to without inadvertently spreading tiny spines through the mash. He used his finger and thumb and dug out some pulp which tasted greener, more vegetal than the fruit. So he was tasting again. A good sign. He banked the slimy pulp around his swollen tongue, swallowing it in tiny gulps, counting to fifteen, then ten between each miniature swallow.

When Hoa had turned and seen that he really wasn't going to make it, her face had taken on a corundum hardness. Maybe she had already made it to the highway now by herself. If she was okay, people would be looking for him soon. If she was okay ... His stomach turned. He touched the top of his head. There was hair there, but he felt scalped. He felt thirstier now than before. He wanted to put his shirt back on. While he was planning what to do next, he passed out.

\* \* \*

It was his long-term complaint that at home, they could never watch a movie together. While he sat in his chair, she would lie on the couch in a harem of pillows and afghans and within thirty minutes, no matter how gripping the movie, she'd be softly snoring. She sounded like a baby alligator. If Dale called her name, her eyes would snap open and she would immediately ask him a question as though she had just been ruminating, with her eyes closed, on some detail in the plot. Did the gigolo take the other guy's coat at the coat check? Were the notebooks blank? What's the name of that actor in the little car, the one playing the mobster? It was remarkable how, in that blink of waking consciousness—with her first, not yet even full breath—she could hatch ingenious questions that were nuanced and perceptive, that Dale had to consider before he could respond. Just the same, it was such an obvious ruse by now that it reminded Dale of the way their old blind beagle, now dead, would sometimes bark at them when they came up the porch steps, and then, realizing her mistake, she'd pretend—no one who has raised dogs doubts that they are capable liars—that she was barking at something behind them, at something which had since disappeared.

*Friday Night*

In his dream, he was part of a small group of guests being led through an expensive Palladian home full of art. In each room, he felt compelled to offer polite comments about bad paintings to the hostess, an immaculately dressed, white-haired woman wearing so much make-up she resembled a bald eagle. Each time he spoke, he saw himself become more diaphanous and phantasmal. And he felt Hoa's eyes burning through him, hating him.

When he woke, the back of his head was pressed to sharp rock, and he was dizzy. He tried to sit straighter, but found he was too weak. Had days or only hours passed? He had the feeling of being somewhere inside the body whose head he looked out from. Through the vertical almond-shaped eye of the cave, he viewed a clean, transparently blue evening. Undulant. He rested his head back against the rock and gathered his breath. He was adrift, but the dizziness was passing. The world began to present to him as though for the first time, glassy and lovely. The evening and all its creatures beat to a single pulse, pounding in the arteries of his throat. Slowly he came to feel his tongue ache and he wondered if he'd bitten it accidentally. Then, as though a huge gear were wheeling into place, engaging his memory, he felt the roiling in his intestines, his throbbing ankle, his sickly dizziness, and the fever chewing his brow.

He managed to sit up against the wall and stare out as the sky buckled in a drama of shifting hues, going pink to red to bruise. Nauseous and serene at once, he decided to watch everything very carefully, to keep a mental record. He needed to pay attention. The details were important for Hoa's sake. Or would be. He thought he heard a distant train, but around him, the cave was lowly rumbling. Something brushed his face, spilling into the twilight. He recoiled, leaning back against the wall and wiping his cheek. There were more. Black shapes expelled from the cave like spadefuls of dirt. Falling lengthwise against the wall, he began to squirm from the cave and the roar.

Flat against the rock beyond the cave's mouth, Dale turned his cheek and squinted at a thrumming inky torrent erupting from somewhere above him, from an invisible portal. He was shaking, everything was shaking, as though he'd fallen to a jet's floor right beside the wing, overcome with thunder and trembling. A few bats continued to shoot out into the night, but the source of the main funnel was elsewhere, some higher egress. The air droned, and the massive funnel forming outside the cave diverged into countercurrents curling off. The rock around Dale seemed to be thumping and squeaking, flapping and rippling through him. Was he coming apart? No, he was breathing. Another breath, slower now.

The bats continued to siphon upward in a vast mass that would drift and reappear like smoke sucked back into a fire. For an endless time he was paralyzed by the din, as the thick hypnotic lariat, twirling in semi-darkness, loosened into the darkness. By the time the clatter diminished into perceptible squeaks, the night was responding with its electronic orchestra of insects, nightbirds, and toads.

Dale wanted to crawl back into the cave, but his colon spasmed, as though the long gush of violence expelled from the cave had stimulated a sympathetic response in his body. He dropped to a knee and bent over. His eyelids were leaden, his scalp and face tingling. Pushing himself to his feet, he limped to the first congregation of mesquite and cacti in the moonlight. The talus was loose, but the slope adjacent to the cave wasn't so steep. By the nopale plant that he had stripped earlier, he undid his belt and pulled his cargo pants and sweaty underwear down, squatting as he faced uphill, holding his hand against the ground for balance. It took all of his concentration to keep from falling over. A few long syrupy spurts erupted as he reached behind on either side to draw his butt cheeks apart. He continued to squat after he knew he was finished. When he raised his head and opened his eyes, he felt wetness at the corners of his eyes leaking down his cheeks. More wasted fluid.

Above his cave, a chimney of rock rose toward a gangly congestion of stars.

*Hoa's Walk*

Leaving Dale behind, Hoa set her eyes ahead, marking in her mind her gait's rhythm. She would keep going at this pace, she told herself, without slowing until she reached paved road. Route 67, north–south. North to Ojinaga. South to wherever she wasn't going. She never looked back for Dale because she would see him soon. That was certain. She put him out of her mind to keep from going crazy, and then she was thinking about him the night before they started on this trip. Before dinner, she had latched onto his neck in the kitchen, sucking briefly at his throat, and told him it was a lamprey kiss. Dale had kissed her back, his lips warm and full, and she'd felt the arousal in her body molding her to him. Something sustaining and real, a substance almost, passed from him into her breasts and belly.

"Baby, sometimes when I think of you I smell different," she said.

He said, "You mean your sense of smell changes?"

"No," she'd answered. "The way I smell."

How many days ago was that?

Her fedora protected her head, but her scalp was swampy. She looked down the trail. Now she needed to put her thirst out of her mind. Visualizing it, she opened the firebox door, set her thirst inside, and shut the door. Now there was only the heat to deal with. It wasn't worse than a firing. She could ignore it. She focused on the highway that must be ahead, but soon she began to hear the repetitive pattern of her footsteps fill in with the four-four witch-you-babe-bee. The same jerky refrain over and over, against her will. She couldn't stop it. Or her gurgling stomach. She was aware of passing many kinds of plants she not only couldn't name, but had never seen before.

*Signs*

The rancid musk woke Dale before he heard anything. It was night. No, his eyes were swollen shut. Why was he sitting up? Then the sound jolted him wholly awake. Something large. Very close. He clutched for his rock and clenched his teeth. The narcos were coming for their stash. It was light enough to see, but nothing entered the cave. What he was hearing turned into a fury of grunts and high squeals. In the cave's ashy mouth, Dale wriggled forward on his belly with the rock in his hand just far enough so he could peer down the slope. A pack of black javelinas—five, six—were shoving each other and shoveling their noses, snorting and snapping in a frenzy. Christ, he thought, it's my shit, that watery shit they're fighting over. Immediately, they sensed him and bolted, weaving down the embankment through the brush. They'll head for water, Dale thought. I can follow their tracks. If Hoa is okay ... I have to get out of here ... *If she's okay* ... Out of here.

He stepped into the dawn without his shirt, shivering at the edge of his cave, collecting himself. The early morning came on without motion, formfast but intensifying. Below, he saw the trail, and on the other side, a steeper slope to flat desert, which stretched to a horizon of dull mountains. There was a thin stroke of dark green he could see to the south. There. Could be. He could get there, he thought. He squeezed his arm and felt it. Good. He swatted his filthy shirt against the wall to clean it off and pulled it on, feeling little cactus spines all along his shoulders. He took off his boots, cargo pants, and underwear. Standing in his shirt and socks, he managed to get his pants back on, sat down, pulled on his boots, and patted the soiled white boxers onto his head like a wilted chef's hat. He felt dizzy, but he thought his ankle was better. If he could make his way back down to the trail without twisting it again. He started for the sluiceway directly below the cave where he would have to negotiate boulders and dead brush, but it looked clearer than any other way down the hill. Here I come, he thought, you rattlesnake motherfuckers.

Hoa walked steadily west and northwest. She stopped only a few times to sit on a broken stone in the shade of some brush, or to rest against an outcrop by the trail. In the late afternoon, she passed a little wooden plank, anchored by stones, on which someone had painted the word *agua*. She almost didn't see it. Off the trail, some twenty feet behind the sign, she spotted a wooden box the size of a microwave. A two-inch plastic pipe angled down from it into a dry rock trough. Sliding the cover back, she found an inch-deep seep-puddle inside, curded with foam and algae. There was no can or ladle or bucket to dip into the water, so Hoa knelt, digging her toes into the dirt for grip while she lowered her face into the box. The water was tepid and scummy. She rested there for half an hour, drinking what she could. Sticking her head in the box. Hoping Dale would catch up with her. Her runner husband.

Before she went on, she arranged a small line of pebbles in the trail, an arrow pointing toward the white agua sign. Dale wouldn't miss it. All afternoon, in a kind of reversal of the myth of Eurydice and Orpheus she thought would appeal to Dale, she looked over her shoulder, but never caught sight of him. He had to be coming. Even on his bad ankle, he could make it this far. He was a runner.

Over and over in her head, as she walked, she imagined him catching up with her, calling her. She pictured the two of them stumbling out onto the dusty paved highway together, a pickup pulling over for them right away. They had been soldered together in love early on, and they had been soldered again in grief. Whatever their lives came to mean after the toll of disappointments and elations, she thought, their bond was a singular thing at the core of who they were, whether separately or together.

Hoa had gone maybe half a mile from the spring box, when she heard a pair of nighthawks trilling like frogs. Her socks had slipped down and bunched into her shoes. She looked up to see that the sun had begun to set. A single vulture drifted across the darkening blue sky like a scrap of ash lofted up from a fire, seesawing ever so slightly above her.

*Leaving the Cave*

Stumbling down the sluiceway from the cave, Dale kept in mind that thin green band of vegetation a mile or so into the desert. It was a sure sign of water. An arroyo. The cactus fruits had helped him, but if he couldn't restore more of his fluids, he was really in trouble. How could Hoa have walked for a day in the sun without water? Where would she have slept? He kept imagining the narcos meeting up with her on their way to the cave, kept forcing himself to come up with positive scenarios. She doesn't threaten them, so they are happy to help her out. They don't want to stir up trouble by killing a gringa. She's in the truck with them headed this way. The variations looped and looped until Dale stood back on the trail again, scratched and bleeding, his ankle throbbing, pulling thin cactus needles from his fingers with his teeth.

He paused about halfway down the second embankment, catching his breath and looking out across the plain below. His head smarted. He could no longer make out the green band of the arroyo he had seen from the cave's mouth. All around him, listing at weird angles to the steep slope, the cactus plants looked like they were about to fall over. There was a hard painful lump in his throat and not enough saliva to swallow it. Some pearl of mucus and dust and acid, he thought, accreting layer over layer, hour by hour, until it plugged up his esophagus. The morning had barely begun, but the sun already sizzled, and the hill, heating up like a loaf of bread, exhaled at him. Dale kept on going down to the plain, kept going, although it seemed impossible. Simple animal effort and reaction. With each crunching step, sand and pebbles shifted under his boots. Flat and puce-colored rock fragments littered the slope and clattered like baked xylophone keys as he made his way around the thorny brush. His vision was blurring.

When Dale had gone a hundred yards or so from the bottom of the slope into the desert, he turned to look behind him. Had he heard Hoa calling his name? His cave had disappeared, winked out from the contours of the volcanic sill. Now, the shape of the mountain behind him was anonymous, unfamiliar. He could just barely perceive the trace of his own descent from the trail, which was only visible as a brush line, a telltale unconformity in the vegetation halfway up the slope. With his right hand, he repetitively and unconsciously rubbed at red stripes and welts on his forearms. His shirt, even though he had shaken it and beaten it against the cave wall to dislodge the fine nopale spines, pricked his shoulders and chest. His fingertips ached. All good, he thought. It was feeling.

Sidestepping a chunk of red-black volcanic rock about the size of his own head, he had an idea. He looked around for another good-sized rock he could lift, unsettled it from the sand, and carried it over to the first rock. Soon, he had assembled a knee-high cairn of three base rocks with a rock on top. Standing next to it, he rechecked his position relative to the slope. He marked a long crevice in the mountain, just east of its highest knob. It would be too easy to drift and lose his way coming back and never find the car again. *Stay found. Stay found.*

He turned back to the desert, mentally projecting a straight line to where he figured he had seen the arroyo from the cave. His eyes were bleary. He turned on his phone, checked the time, and turned it off again. He could walk for an hour at most. If he didn't find the arroyo by then, he would be wasting his energy. For the next forty minutes, he sighted ahead to a century plant, a spray of ocotillo, a cactus, leaving at each subsequent site increasingly smaller cairns. As he walked, he flattened the underwear over his head and pulled the legs over his ears. The sun was unrelenting, the desert so silent, each of his steps exploded beneath him. It was like hearing himself chewing an apple into a microphone.

Whenever Dale closed his eyes, an expanding yellow circle appeared behind his eyelids. Even though he was dehydrated, he felt bloated. He stopped and checked behind him again. If he got lost, that would be it. The crevice in the ever more remote cliff face was still visible, still marking his return to the trail and the car. He pulled up the bottom of his pants and examined his right knee. There were bruises and lacerations across it, and underneath the kneecap, a nasty boil had formed.

Dale put together three stones and realigned himself facing south. Ahead of him, the brush thickened. He guessed he had come about three miles from the trail.

The arroyo wasn't visible through the green sea of chest-high mesquite, but he knew it was there. So he walked west, looking for an animal trail through the thicket. Somewhere, the javelinas must have plowed a tunnel to the streambed. The sun was blaring, and after a few minutes, he decided he had no choice, his time was running out. Straight into the rampant mesquite he plunged.

## The Arroyo and Back

As he waded twenty, thirty, fifty feet into the mesquite, it gave way to fan-spray yuccas and sotols and century plants edging a precipitous bajada that was fenestrated with the holes of pocket mice. Dale halted and peered down from the crumbly lip, his cheeks, torso, and arms bleeding. Below him, he could see a dry alluvial flat, its sand rippled by past torrents. It stretched south into the wide desert glimmering with heat.

From the scarp of the bajada, Dale took a few test steps into the loose sand and half slid, half plummeted down into the arroyo, trying to bear the brunt on his good foot, his boots sinking deep in the soft slope with each step. At the bottom, he brushed sand from his pants, and was amazed that he hadn't re-injured his ankle. It would be easy to find his way back here, he thought, looking at his glide mark in the bajada's flank. He sat down to take off his boots and tap out the sand. While he was putting them back on, a long gray-brown snake tongued its way past him on the far side of the dry river bed, disappearing into a depression like a wrinkle tugged flat in the sand itself.

Dale took it for a sign. He stood up and followed. The snake seemed impervious to his presence. Both snake and man stayed close to the bajada slope, the snake rippling ahead, faster than Dale could hobble, but then pausing and testing the air with its tongue. Dale was never closer than twenty feet before it zipped from sight, only to reappear ahead of him. Folds and runnels crisscrossed the sand in the old riverbed like lines in a hand, the snake pouring itself into and out of them.

At the top of the bajada on Dale's left, a squalor of spiky greenery cast a weak shadow onto the slope. The sweat-wet underwear covered his head, but Dale still felt the sun blowtorching the back of his neck. Beneath his boots, the composition of sand was changing. It went white as talcum, then it darkened and pebbled. The snake was gone. Dale dropped onto his bruised knees in a little bend where the shadow from above almost reached, and he began to dig into the sand with his fingers. Under the fine top layer of sand, a grainier substratum tore his already raw fingertips. He managed about six inches or so before getting up and continuing to limp in the direction the frozen ripple patterns indicated was downstream. How long had he been walking? How much time had he lost?

* * *

During their relationship, Dale and Hoa had both become more interested in plants, in the names of trees and weeds and flowers. Dale had assiduously studied Hoa's field books and slowly mastered distinctions that he quickly forgot again as the seasons changed and the years passed. But the names stuck with Hoa. On their walks, she would notice flowering plants and occasionally remark on them. Her commentaries weren't the straightforward identification feats that he had practiced, which would lead him to casually call out *cottonwood* or *red mulberry*. She was more likely to pluck a leaf from a tree they passed and say, Swallowtails love these leaves. He'd say, What is it?, and she'd look at the leaf and say,

Toothache tree, it's a pepperbark. Hoa touched plants the way she touched clay or stray cats, as if each were her lost pet. Always with a reflective, lavish gentleness.

* * *

At the point Dale decided he couldn't afford to turn back to the trail, he noticed a discoloration in the sand up ahead. He trudged forward to find two holes and two piles of loose sand crisscrossed by tracks—coyote, dog? Both holes were narrow, dug down at least a foot, and at the bottom of each, he saw water. He threw himself down on all fours in the scratched sand and sniffed at the holes. He couldn't smell anything, but there were no dead bugs. He looked carefully, steadying himself. The right sign, he thought. He lay down on his belly. There was just enough space for him to lower his head into the wider hole. He knocked sand into the little pool with his cheeks and his forehead and then his shoulder, the air turning to earth, the earth turning to water, and he shut his eyes, sucking up a mouthful of watery sand, swallowing it in small gulps, keeping his head in the hole in a painfully stressed position, and trying to move as little as possible.

When Dale found his way back to the cairns, it was evening. Tremors of desperation or ecstasy or fever were shivering up the back of his neck. He felt like he had been limping for weeks. The little rock heaps helped him, and when he reached the last one—the first that he'd made—he felt a surprising urge to pee. He peed against the cairn, a little stream of urine the color of cola. Then, at the bottom of the slope, he bent forward from the waist, leaning like the twisted cholla and barrel cacti, using scrub bushes for handholds. He told himself he would not stop ascending until he made the trail.

He had lugged himself partway up the slope when he heard something. Maybe sensed it before he heard it. He paused and shaded his eyes with his hand. Thirty feet above him, a hedge of ocotillo and mesquite marked the trail's edge. He wasn't going up the slope on the same trajectory that he had come down, so he wasn't sure if he would be closer to the cave or the car when he reached the trail. When he heard a man's voice, faint, at a distance, a chill and a hope went through him at the same time. Dale was completely exposed coming up the hill. Anyone who stood at the edge of the trail and looked down would see him immediately, his silly white underwear hat. Even if he got to the thicker brush adjacent to the trail, it would be tricky to stay hidden. He hunched low and ascended the last fifteen feet holding his breath, terrified he would slide again or make a noise. For the last five feet, he was crawling between clumps of grass and scraggly mesquite. Low branches tripped him and thorns ripped his ankles. He jammed the upper part of his knee, the same knee with the boil, into a little barrel cactus and couldn't believe the clarity of the pain.

What were the chances the men would be with Hoa, come to help?

He peered out from behind the bush, his face low to the sand. His head was killing him. A metallic blue pickup was coming from the east, toward him. And it was towing his rental car. Good sign, right? Inertia held him in place. The truck stopped a stone's throw away. He couldn't see his rental car behind the truck now but he heard the car door open and shut. A young man appeared in the middle of the trail behind the pickup. He had a thin mustache and wore a long-sleeved blue patterned shirt and a hemp-colored gaucho hat with a round rim.

Then the door to the pickup opened and another man stepped out onto the trail.

The two men met between the vehicles and spoke to each other, gazing at the upper slope. The man closest to Dale, the one he saw exiting the pickup, seemed to have a strange tick. His head bobbed on his neck as though he were constantly catching himself from falling asleep. He was wearing jeans and boots. The sides of his white cowboy hat curved up against the crown. He went around the back of the truck and dropped the tailgate. They both disappeared behind the truck and reappeared in the brush in the sluiceway going up toward the cave. They were gone in the creosote, and then Dale caught a glimpse of them again, moving upward much more quickly than Dale had managed to come down the same way.

Dale didn't see many options. The pickup was facing away from Sierra Mojada, but that didn't mean the narcos had come from there. They might have come from route 67 and turned around when they tied the rental car to the truck. He couldn't make out any tire tracks, but he didn't have a good angle looking through the brush. If they had come from Sierra Mojada, they wouldn't have crossed paths with Hoa as she trudged her way to route 67. That was good. But they were heading toward route 67 now, with the rental car in tow. That meant everything bad. If Hoa hadn't reached the highway yet or was lost or had turned back, they would run into her.

Dale saw both men emerge from the cave—the guy with the waggling head in front of the young guy with the mustache—with shiny brown packages the size of carry-on luggage under each arm. That's going to be hard, Dale thought, coming down that sluice carrying that stuff. They disappeared from Dale's sight and less than ten minutes later, the bob-head stepped out of the creosote onto the trail right behind his truck. He dumped the packages onto the lowered gate and climbed in, readjusting them in the bed near the cab. The younger guy showed up behind him, looking like maybe he'd fallen. He was disheveled, his gold chain hanging outside his shirt and his hat jammed low on his forehead.

The two men didn't speak. The younger one put his packages into the truck bed and Bob-head moved them beside the others.

Then, both went back up the sluice to the cave and came down again loaded the same way. The fifth or sixth time they went up, Dale backed out of the brush, dropping down the precipice about ten feet. He weaved his way closer to the truck, and when he was about parallel with it, he wedged his way between bushes, lying on the ground, and waited there without even the beginning of a plan.

He could slip into the back of the rental car and hide on the floor. No one ever looked in the backseat when he got in to drive. But what then? Even if he put a choke hold on the skinny guy at the wheel and squeezed until he passed out, there'd be only one chance to get it right and he'd still be in a car attached to the bob-head's truck. He'd be entirely visible in the truck's rearview mirror.

* * *

The two men carried packages out of the cave for almost two hours. Steadily, without rest. Shadow darkened the sluiceway now as the sun dropped toward the horizon. In the meantime, Dale's breath had gone out of him. There was sand and dust in his mouth and eyes. He almost closed them.

Bob-head got into the bed of the truck and made some adjustments to the packages, while Mustache made a solo trip back up to the cave. Dale's attention was drawn back to the truck. Was that a soccer ball? Bob-head was picking up soccer balls from the truck bed. There were five or six of them. He was distributing them like spacers between the stacked packages. When Mustache emerged from the creosote bushes, handing his two packages over the back of the truck, they spoke to each other, but Dale couldn't make out what they said. Mustache got into the passenger side of the truck and Bob-head hopped to the ground, coming around and sliding behind the wheel. The truck started up.

This is it, Dale thought. It's now or never. His right hand was trembling.

* * *

All but paralyzed with tension, Dale fixed his eyes on the door of the truck. He had a rock the size of a pear in his right hand and he was squeezing a smaller shard of chert in his left.

He had slid furtively along the line of brush far enough to see that the rental car's cross-member was tied to the truck's rear bumper with about six feet of knotted red strap—the Prizm seatbelts. The two men sat in the cab as the western sky began to reflect against the windshield. Dale could see both caves, the one he had spent the night in and the small inaccessible one above it. The one the bats used. Over the rock rim, the air was blue and darkening. The men were smoking with their windows down. How are they going to tow the car with both of them in the fucking truck? Dale asked himself. Who's going to keep the car on the trail?

He was shuffling through the possibilities, far-fetched as they were. If he stayed in place and did nothing, his chances weren't good. And Hoa might be in serious trouble. He imagined leaping from his hiding place as the rental car got pulled past him, throwing himself onto the trunk in a balletic way. It was getting dark. And then he tried to imagine himself holding onto the trunk as the car got towed to the highway. There was no way he had that much strength or quickness.

Bob-head's door opened and Dale heard the truck engine cut. Both the man and his partner got out. What was this now? They were coming to find him. Dale glanced down the trail in the direction of Sierra Mojada. There was nothing to run toward, not that he could run. His only chance was diving down the cactus slope below, trying to get behind some cover lower down. He looked west, up the trail, and there was Hoa in her white short-sleeved shirt, walking around the bend in the twilight.

He couldn't make out her face, but her hair was a mess and her posture was off-kilter, her face held up, angled like she was trying to read something in Vietnamese. Jesus Christ. Terrified, he looked at the Mexicans, but they hadn't seen her. They were already through the bushes, starting up the sluice toward the cave again.

*Hoa's Turn*

Hoa hadn't reached the highway. After hiking six or seven hours, she agonized about turning back. The pace of her walking slowed, but a kind of frenzy took hold of her. Dire scenes howled through her mind.

As long as she went west, it was impossible that she'd miss the highway. Yet, before twilight, alone, in the middle of a desert, she made a decision to leave the trail. It must have been bending north the whole time, that was the only explanation for why she hadn't reached the highway. She checked herself against the sun and tried to walk as straight west as she could for two more hours. It was slow going. Over slippery, lichen-covered slabs of rock, between vicious clumps of shrubs, along dead floodways and up snakey hills, she thought she picked up sections of animal trails, mule deer, or javelinas, but they faded out each time. She was having to make her way so slowly through the terrain, divagating around so many obstacles, she was afraid of losing her bearings altogether. As the sun dropped lower, she reached a rise and stood, rocking slightly in the long day's heat like a vase in a fire. She stared out at an unordered wilderness. She did not want to come together with it. If only there were a sign of some kind, some sign of presence or direction. The exposed skin of her arms had burned. Her heart was pounding as though she'd been running full out for miles. She wasn't going to reach the highway. She felt something begin to crack inside herself. She almost broke.

And then she hardened.

By twilight, she made her way back to the trail and she lay down in the rut. She passed the night between bouts of foreboding and the kind of sleep in which she dreamed she was awake, lying there unsleeping. She was absolutely certain now that she should have gone south where the trail first split.

The next day, when she finally reached that fork in the trail again, she realized that Dale and the car were only a few miles further east. She kept going back. She prayed she would run into Dale, that he was limping her way. But after trudging in his direction for a while, she knew he had stayed at the car or gone to the cave he'd pointed out. Or he'd already taken the southern fork and come out at the highway with no idea that she was still wandering. Her damp fedora shaded her brow, but she kept her eyes fixed on the trail in front of her. Her knees ached and her feet were blistered. When she saw the pickup truck and two men in hats climbing out of the cab, she almost broke into a run. She didn't spot Dale anywhere and her pace slowed, but she couldn't stop walking forward. The two men in hats — or was it a man and a boy? — stepped off the trail. She kept on stumbling forward like a wind-up toy. It was getting dark, but she saw the men reappear higher up the slope, one behind the other, climbing. Amber sunbeams lit up sections of the ridge.

Then Hoa stopped dead in her tracks. She was still fifty yards away. Dale — it was clearly Dale and yet there was something wrong with him — emerged in a crouch from the side of the trail. What did he have on his head? He glanced toward her once — had he actually seen her? And then he opened the truck's door and leaned into the cab. He was hidden by the door. She couldn't see what he was doing. But then she saw him hobble behind the truck. Bent forward like an old man with a bad back. Their red rental car was behind the truck. Dale opened the car door, got in and out again, minus whatever he'd been wearing on his head, and limped back to the truck. She had never seen him move like that. Such wounded animal ferocity. She held up, frozen. Until she heard shouting. One of the men who had gone up the escarpment was shouting. She heard an engine rev, and the blue pickup lurched forward, Dale behind the wheel, and she heard a gunshot, three gunshots. Four.

\* \* \*

The truck's engine wound so high in first gear, it was screaming. Dale let out the clutch, and the truck scrabbled straight toward Hoa. When it slowed, the rental car slammed into the back of it and the nose of the truck lurched forward, slewing to the left and almost knocking her off the trail.

"Get into the car and steer," Dale called thinly, sticking his head from the open window of the cab. She couldn't move. His face was scratched and purple and terrible, a purgatorial counter of itself. There was cold intent in his eyes. He opened the truck door. "Get into the car and steer," he screamed hoarsely. "Keep it in neutral!"

She heard another gunshot. She couldn't recall moving but then she was at the Prizm, ripping open the door and sliding behind the wheel. Dale revved the truck again, the car jerked forward, and Hoa almost fell out through the open door. She grabbed the steering wheel with her right hand and yanked the door closed, her deadened right foot testing the brake. She aimed the car right behind the truck. The seatbelt chime was going off, but she couldn't find her seatbelt. As they rounded the first turn in the trail, the truck's taillights came on. The hills were swallowing the sun.

\* \* \*

Thirty minutes later, when they came to the fork where Hoa had walked northwest to nowhere, she honked the car horn. Dale was driving slowly anyway, trying to keep the towrope taut, and when he stopped, Hoa pressed the brakes. She put the car in park and ran up to the truck. Dale looked even worse closer up. The hard landscape—its scars and rifts and dust—had entered his face, taking it over. He was as carved and rindled as the volcanic rocks, weird and ancient, his eyes squinty and red. He looked reptilian, his forehead bubbled, his lips smeared with white film. His expression was unrecognizable to her.

Dale said something first, but she couldn't understand him, so she simply flung herself at him.

"What happened?" She was crying uncontrollably, shivering. Happy.

He pushed her off. "Can you keep driving?" His voice was squashed and cold. She looked at the ghastliness of her husband, the purple vascular bundles in his cheeks, and she swallowed. "Yes," she said, still leaning into the truck, trying to bury her face in his chest. "Yes. But let's just take the truck and leave the car."

"We've got to get out of here," Dale said. "They're making calls."

"There's no reception," Hoa blubbered, letting him go, stepping back to look at him again. He didn't sound right.

"We can't untie the seatbelts. They're knotted up tight, there's nothing to cut them with."

As suddenly as she had started, she stopped crying and looked up the trail. "We have to go left up here," she said more firmly. "South. I walked the other way and it goes nowhere."

She turned back to him. "Baby, what happened to you?"

"We get to 67, we'll be okay," he said.

He looked like he'd been run over. A couple of times. And dragged.

Then she saw something flicker in his face, as though he were just now focusing on her. "You made it," he said, his eyes welling. He was shaking all over.

She raised up on her toes and leaned forward again through the open door, smashing her face into his shoulder, his sullied shirt, reaching up blindly with her fingers for his face. He pressed his hand against her cheek but didn't say anything. Then she stepped back and jogged to the car, sliding in, racking the seat forward, and shifting into neutral. The seatbelt chime started up again. Dale's grungy once-white boxer shorts were in the seat next to her.

Then Dale was getting out of the truck. He came limping around the back and let down the tailgate. When she saw what he was doing, she put the Prizm in park again and got out, climbing up into the truck bed to help him. The packages were weighty, caked with dust.

"Jesus Christ," she said. "Bar codes?"

She lifted the end of one of the shiny brown packages, flopped it upright against the bedrail, then she lifted the bottom end and dropped it over the side of the truck into the dirt. The packages were compressed and heavy, each with a white bar code taped to the plastic. It took the two of them a few minutes to clear the truck bed of everything but the soccer balls. Dale bent down and scooped up the balls one at a time and tossed then into the desert.

No more words passed between them.

Then Hoa said, "Go."

* * *

The next three quarters of an hour, in moonlight, in tandem, the filthy Prizm lashed to the Dodge pickup, they bounced up and down through potholes, crossed a cattle guard, and passed a boarded-up shack. Whenever Hoa touched the brakes, they squealed. She used Dale's boxer shorts to wipe the dust from the inside of the windshield. They snaked their way through the foothills, dropping into gullies and ravines, and coming up the far banks slowly in first gear. Dale started slapping himself hard to keep from falling asleep, but he barely felt the slaps. It was like hearing them happen to someone else. He ran the truck's windshield wipers to clear the phosphorescence from the windshield. Then the first little adobe house appeared. The trail emptied itself into a wider, packed-dirt road.

They rounded a switchback, and Hoa heard a mule braying. There were palo verde pens and several adobe houses. Hoa kept the car lights off, her eyes trained on the red-lit back of the truck, seeing snatches of whatever the truck's headlights illuminated. A store on the left. A hound yowling on a chain. It felt to her like they were traveling in some altered time. Her flesh was chalky, and in the rearview mirror, in the darkness, she saw a surreal glimmering phantom of herself. And the living, where were they?

*Sunday Morning*

They parked on the street across from a closed Pemex station around three in the morning. Dale slept upright against the door, while Hoa, next to him in the truck, kept watch. She stared at the industrial plant and the fires on its flare stacks a mile or so to the north. At five a.m. the office light in the gas station came on. Hoa waited until she saw a car pull alongside the pumps before she woke Dale.

Dale gassed up while Hoa went inside. In the fluorescent brightness, the man at the register looked unreal to Hoa. Then she caught a reflection of herself in the sliding-glass doors to the cold drinks and she realized that she looked far worse. She bought six bottles of a red sports water and some pastries, but when she pulled one out of the bag at the gas pump, Dale said he couldn't eat it.

The attendant came out and Dale paid for the gas with sweat-soaked peso notes from his wallet. While Hoa laid four of the sports drinks on the cab bench, Dale opened the trunk. Their duffel bags were still there. He unzipped the inner pockets and took out their passports. The air reeked of diesel fuel. Up the road, toward the exit ramp, Dale saw sixteen-wheelers lined up end to end facing north like paralyzed caterpillars on a branch.

"You need to eat something," Hoa said. "And maybe we could get the car fixed here."

"Not on Sunday," Dale said. "Presidio. We get across the Ojinaga Presidio bridge and then we're safe."

Dale slammed the Prizm's trunk and stepped into the space between the truck and the car. There were handprints where the tailgate had been raised and lowered, and he smudged them away with the bottom of his shirt. Next, he squatted and checked the knots in the seatbelt towropes. Hoa noticed that the numbers and letters of the license plates of both vehicles were caked with filth, completely unreadable.

"Without anyone recognizing this truck. Before those guys get word out," Dale said.

Hoa thought Dale looked at least ten years older. He was repeating himself, too. How were those guys at the cave going to get word out without a car or phone reception, but she didn't say anything. If Dale needed to cross the border now, they were going to cross the border now.

"We get the car fixed here—" he was down on his hands and knees studying the underchassis of the car in the bad light—"people see us. We pay with a credit card, they find out who we are and where we live."

The car behind them at the pumps honked.

"Hand me the charger," he said outside her window. She reached for the console, and he pulled his phone from his pocket and turned it on.

"The drinks are in your seat, Dale," she said.

For the next hour, Hoa was stabbed by the sun coming through her windshield. The sky was light blue with gorgeous clouds and shafts of light gleaming down between. As they came into Ojinaga on Avenida Libre Comercio, the traffic backed up. Despite that they were in different vehicles, Dale's paranoia worked its way into her. Slowed up in the congestion, conspicuously being towed, she felt visible, vulnerable. A yellow bus ahead flashed its lights, letting out a dozen girls carrying identical metal lunchboxes. A few adults in neon-orange shirts waited to escort them across the two-lane.

One car had scraped another at an intersection and a bottleneck in both directions had formed. Car horns were bleating from both ends of the tangle. The cars involved in the accident didn't move, no one got out of either one, but the traffic began to flow around them on either side. At the next stoplight, a street vendor hawking T-shirts pressed Dale to buy one. Three boys spilled over to Hoa's window, chanting to wash her windshield. She reached into her pocket, pulling out a small wad of dollars, giving one to the first boy, another to the second. They had started washing only her side before the light changed and the truck tugged the car forward. Dale was getting better at this. He could see the cars ahead queuing into two lanes for the bridge.

The inspection station was an open-air bay under a long tin roof, and the Mexican officers passed them through. Just ahead were the toll booths. Dale went to take another sip from the last of his bottles, but it was empty. He tossed it into the footwell. His phone was charging in the passenger seat. He picked it up. Searching, searching. A signal. Presidio was just across the bridge. One missed call. From Declan. Dale glanced at Hoa in the rearview mirror, her head turned toward the shops on the left side of the street.

They passed a sign that said *Puesto de Control Militar* and Dale pulled into the far-right lane. Tinny brass radio music mixed with the calls of hawkers and the grainy hum and percussion of idling engines and bad mufflers. Vendors in bicycle carts were selling iced drinks. A man with long hair and a knapsack held out a can of Coke, walking the line of cars and trucks. Dale was afraid to make eye contact. From the tin and glass of tiendas, from the hoods and windows of cars, the sun's glare spindled into sharp beams.

Up ahead, Dale could see pedestrians walking into Mexico along the covered left corridor of the bridge. On the right side, a crowd stood behind three barred gates. A few Federales in black uniforms were striding back and forth between the lines of cars and the steel barrels and orange cones that blocked the middle lane. The brake lights of the car in front of Dale flashed faintly on and off in the hard sun. Dale held his breath. He could see the rise of the bridge through the concrete portico. Just before the tollbooth, there was a cluster of men in neon-orange road-crew vests carrying white buckets. One of them approached his open window sucking a lime, spitting the seeds into his hand. Dale looked away and adjusted the rearview mirror.

"Para las mujeres," said the man in the orange vest standing at his cab window.

"What women?" Dale asked, turning his ravaged face toward the man.

Unperturbed by Dale's appearance, the man pointed ahead of him at the pier in the main arch of the tollbooths. A massive pink wooden sculpture was assembled there in the shape of a cross, hammered with oversized nails from which hung purses and necklaces and high heels and tags with women's names. Jessica Morales, Marcela Fernández, Verónica Beltrán, Maria Irma Plancarte ... On the ground in front of the cross was a mannequin with its breasts cut away.

"God," Dale gasped.

"Las que mataron," the man said solemnly.

Dale fumbled to extract his wallet. After paying for his gas earlier, he'd counted sixty-three U.S. dollars and only a few more pesos. He took out a ten and gave it to the man, who dropped the seeds in his hand and nodded, saying in English with almost no accent, "Happy Father's Day." Dale took his foot off the brake and immediately jammed it down again. Behind him, the Prizm rammed the bumper of the truck. An old woman passed crossways in front of him carrying on her back a basket of avocados lashed to her forehead with a tumpline. Beside her were two young girls toting plastic shopping bags, loaded with things that banged against their calves.

Dale fell asleep and jerked awake, but no time had passed. He glanced in the rearview, and there was Hoa, alert, watching through the windshield, steady on. He felt a knot in his solar plexus melt, waves of emotion radiating into his torso. He adjusted the mirror and caught a glimpse of himself. He looked like a wildman, a Neanderthal, but for the first time in untold hours, he thought he was going to live. His face was beet-red and there were tear tracks in the grime on his cheeks. He paid the man at the toll with American dollars and added a twenty-dollar bill, explaining that their car had broken down. No problem, no problem, the Mexican toll keeper assured him, looking up from the bills. When he got to the American side, the toll taker added, he should pull over into the secondary inspection area. The border patrol might let him call a tow truck.

Dale thanked the man, the beautiful pock-faced man. He let out the clutch and yanked the rental car through the booth. Midway across the bridge, Dale looked right and left and saw the placid brown river and its little islands of trees.

His phone vibrated against his thigh and rang.

*epilogue*

Wearing a sombrero, he rides a horse smaller than the one on which he entered Mexico. He spurs it south from Chihuahua City after posting his letter to Carrie. The dirt road from Chihuahua to Delicias and further southeast all the way to Escalon is tolerable. But already, it's been a long ride for a man in his seventies. In Escalon, Bierce rests and drinks, but turns down dinner. The next morning, he points his horse northeast into the desert and keeps field-side of the railroad tracks. Some ten miles on, spikes and tie plates are rooted up and the ballast dug away. The track is busted, the rails splayed outward like the antennae of a centipede. Here the horse's hooves begin to unearth and kick forward pale fossil shells in clouds of pale dust. The remaining railroad tracks stretch across scrubland toward the mountains where, beyond a few fenced ranches, they slip through a circuitous pass into Sierra Mojada. He walks the horse by a dozen identical miners' houses separated by empty palo verde pens. Men are conducting afternoon business outside one- and two-story adobe buildings along a main dirt street that leads — Bierce lifts the brim of his sombrero — toward a cemetery maybe a quarter mile away. Bierce has heard from a reliable source that a band of Federales has taken control of Sierra Mojada, threatening the two American superintendents of the mining company. If they try to leave, or if any miners escape to join Villa, they will be hunted down and shot. But that doesn't worry him.

Bierce is a few days ahead of Villa's troops, anticipating that something might play out here in the lee of a four-thousand-foot massif from which someone can see to the National Railway and seventy miles in any direction. He is a tired man on a tired horse. He unmounts at an adobe hovel and goes inside, paying for a bottle, claiming an empty table with four chairs. He drags one chair a foot away from the table, then pulls out another and sits down, putting his boots up on the seat of the first one. The vamps are slathered in dust, but the boot shafts are oily brown where his cuffs have risen. He grumbles to himself. None of the Federales in the bar is wearing a uniform. They keep an eye on the gringo as he smooths out maps on the table, sketching in trails from his notes, and asking gruff questions of the bartender in a language that is incomprehensible except when he uses the word Villa. He uses it again. And again. Outside the bar, two boys unhitch Bierce's little horse from the post and lead it into another future.

When they are certain that the old man is alone, not simply ahead of his party, a half-dozen Federales approach the table. The drunkest man in the room, hat in hand, lurches directly up to Bierce, asking questions in Spanish and spitting incidentally. When Bierce gazes up into his glassy eyes, he sees all of the men closing in. The only word he understands is Villa and he hears it again and again. Yes, Villa, he answers. I want to see Villa. Two young men on each side stand him up, each gripping an arm and twisting it behind his back.

He notices that his horse is gone as they shove and then drag him out of the bar, down the dirt path toward the cemetery. A gang of boys is skipping behind. There is some discussion at the cemetery's entrance before Bierce is hustled along the waist-high adobe wall to its southeast corner where the dirt is strewn with white rocks. Sweating, Bierce is barking the words "Journalista" and "Americano," but the Mexicans are all arguing with each other.

He pushes back against them and shouts with all the military authority he can muster. "Americano. Journalista."

But the men are already sliding like water spiders away from him, and he is alone, stone-like, ancient, immobile, exhausted, his back to the adobe wall. He half sits against the edge. He takes off his sombrero and settles it on the capstone. His palm flat over the brim. Shifting his weight a little, he looks from one to the other of the two soldiers' single open eyes, no more than fifteen feet from him, aiming through the inverted V-blades of their long barrels at his chest.

*acknowledgments*

Thanks to the John Simon Guggenheim Foundation for a fellow-ship supporting this work. Thanks to the Rockefeller Fellowship from United States Artists that allowed me time to work on this book.

Thanks to the Lannan Foundation for a residency at Marfa, Texas.

Thanks to the Squaw Valley Writers Conference, where I wrote the poems appearing in this book.

Thanks to John Balaban and Brian Turner for the Ojinaga & Closed Canyon adventures.

Thanks to Ashwini Bhat, whose ceramic sculptures can be seen at ashwinibhat.com.

Thanks to David Gottesman.

Thanks to Professor Jerry Johnson of University of Texas at El Paso and his herpetology students, Tony Gandara, Steven Dilks, Art Rocha, and Vicente Mata-Silva.

Grateful acknowledgment to Don Swaim for keeping active an Ambrose Bierce website and to Leon Day for his fanatical research into the death of Bierce, from which I have borrowed.

Thanks to the late Padre James Lienert for sharing his stories of serving as pastor in the desert communities around Sierra Mojada.